A ROMP THROUGH TIME, SPACE, AND ANCIENT ROME

Two award-winning writers take us on an alternate history adventure—a 1940s barnstorming baseball team, led by retired baseball player and spy Moe Berg, is transported from rural Illinois to Ancient Rome, just after the death of Emperor Septimius Severus.

The Romans—who actually played a game called "small ball"—put the captured team to work teaching baseball to the gladiators for a major Colosseum event ... that turns into an over-the-top, life or death finale.

Baseball hijinks, a wild ride through Rome in a careening team bus, a hint of romance, and some viciously good hitting and fielding.

Will the Wandering Warriors make it home? Will the widowed empress escape the fate her evil son has in mind for her? Will the rattletrap team bus make its way through time and space (and Roman roads) back to Illinois?

Will Chicago White Sox owner Grace Comiskey show up to make an unlikely offer to the team's best player?

THE WANDERING WARRIORS

INCLUDES TWO BONUS STORIES

ALAN SMALE

RICK WILBER

WFP
WORDFIRE PRESS

Cover design by Alejandro Colucci
Cover artwork images by Alejandro Colucci
Kevin J. Anderson, Art Director
Published by
WordFire Press, LLC
PO Box 1840
Monument CO 80132
Kevin J. Anderson & Rebecca Moesta, Publishers
WordFire Press eBook Edition 2020
WordFire Press Trade Paperback Edition 2020
WordFire Press Hardcover Edition 2020
Printed in the USA
Join our WordFire Press Readers Group for
sneak previews, updates, new projects, and giveaways.
Sign up at wordfirepress.com

DEDICATIONS

This book is dedicated to Professor Robin S. Wilber, Ph.D., aka the brains of the outfit. Robin is my wife and best friend, my patient and skillful first-reader for all my stories despite her busy schedule as a Professor of Finance at St Petersburg College, and a tireless runner and cyclist who sets the pace for the rest of the family. — Rick Wilber

To my wife, Karen Smale; my parents, Peter and Jill Smale; and the many other fine companions in my travels through the years. Propino tibi salutem! — Alan Smale

THE WANDERING
WARRIORS

ALAN SMALE AND RICK WILBER

1

JULY 1946

It was a steamy July night. We were filling up the tank of our old Ford Transit bus at Ambler's Texaco in Dwight, Illinois, when Quentin Williams, one of our two "Cubans" on the Warriors, had the great idea of getting off the dependable concrete of Route 66 and taking the back roads down to Decatur.

We were all standing around, some of the players smoking and a few spitting out tobacco juice from their chaw while a few of us—me, included—drank cold pop from the station's icebox. Sure, we were tired. The doubleheader on Sunday had gone extra innings both games, and we'd finally had to call the second game a draw when it got too dark to play—ten hours of baseball on a hot Illinois summer day that had started at noon and ended with us driving off into the darkness. And all for a total of maybe two hundred bucks, split eleven ways. But that's how it was for the Wandering Warriors.

I was stiff and my knees were sore after a full day catching, so I was a little disagreeable. As I opened up the side hood to tinker with the distributor cap, I said I wasn't sure it was a great idea to get off the main road and drive through the night on narrow two-lane blacktop. I mentioned that a wrong turn or two and we might wind up in Indiana or Missouri or anywhere else and then we'd have to spend all morning driving back to where we were supposed to be in time for the noon game in Decatur. And the Decatur Dukes were supposed to be pretty good this year, and so were we, so there'd be a nice crowd. We'd make three or four times as much money as we had in Kankakee. Let's play it safe, I said, and stick to the main highway.

Then I slammed the hood down, climbed into the driver's seat, and turned the key to start up the old Transit. It backfired once—the distributor cap still wasn't quite right—and then settled into a nice rumble.

"Professor," Quentin said from the front row behind me, laughing, "you got no sense of adventure. Plus," he said, "this will get us to that hotel in Decatur an hour faster, so we can get some sleep before we do this all over again tomorrow."

Quentin liked the Prairie Hotel in Decatur because our two "Cubans" and our two Jews—me being one of them—got rooms with no trouble there. It wasn't like that in some of the towns we played in farther south. Sure, the Major Leagues broke the color line during the war when the Negro vets started coming home. But at the level we played and the towns we played in, it wasn't so simple as that.

There were little mumblings of agreement in the back of the bus. Quentin loved maps and thought of himself as our navigator, and the guys trusted him. He was smart as a whip. Hell, like me, he even read the newspaper every day, which really impressed the guys. Plus, a shorter drive and more sleep sounded good to the Wandering Warriors.

I sighed and rolled my eyes and said, "Quentin, I'll talk to the driver, but that map of yours better get us there in the dark." He laughed. I was the driver. And the owner. And the catcher. Quentin was our ace and he'd won sixteen on the season. We had a good understanding. I laughed with him, and about five miles down Route 66, I took a left when Quentin said to, and that's how it all began.

( )

At first the road was fine, two-lane and not wide; but it was paved and there was no traffic, so we moved along at a pretty decent clip, fields of knee-high corn on both sides of this good farmland. Every now and then, the road curved and the head-lights would pick out a farmhouse or a barn in the distance, but mostly we saw telephone poles and corn. Lots of corn. And the land was flat as a pancake, the way Illinois can be.

The road wound its way south, and us with it, for nearly an hour before Quentin said to me, "Take a right up there, Profes-sor," and next road I saw, I did just that. It was narrower, but still paved. The old Ford occupied most of that concrete. We'd have had to pull over and squeeze by if there'd been anybody coming the other way; but there wasn't, just fields of wheat now in the headlights, and some soybeans here and there, a mist rising from the fields as it started to sneak up on midnight.

I liked driving the bus, even at night on back roads in Illi-nois. Being on the road was necessary to the game I spent all summer playing, like a child; and driving the bus was part and parcel with catching and hitting and running the bases: a comfort, a happiness. I'd played the game for money when I was younger, and I'd done all right, though in my naïveté I hadn't realized what it all meant. Then the war had come, and I'd done what they asked of me—odd and mysterious though it often was —and when it was over, so was my career as a spy and as a ballplayer. So now I played for the joy of it. I didn't dare tell my players any of this. They'd have ribbed me unmercifully.

I'd always been a good backstop as a kid in St. Louis; soft hands, strong arm, good hitting. I played for University City High School, where I was head of the class in school as well as sports, and did well enough to be the starting catcher for the college nine at Washington U. there in St. Louis, where I took my degree in Literature and then sailed through the doctorate in Classical Languages. Then, at twenty-five, I showed up at a tryout in Springfield, Illinois, and they gave me a contract, catchers being hard to find. In three years, I climbed through the minors and on to the big club, the competition tougher at every level, so I went from star to starter to journeyman; but I made the team, a backup catcher for the White Sox. That's where I stayed for six good years, playing in fifty or sixty games a season, hitting a respectable mid two-hundreds, handling a favorite pitcher or two. Good glove, not much of an arm, decent bat but not enough power. Solid. That was me, and I was happy to be there. The Professor, the guys called me when a local reporter caught on to my education, and the nickname stuck.

And then came the war, and I wound up working in Intelligence on one little island after another as we fought our way to Japan. I spoke Japanese, and that made me useful as an interrogator when we had prisoners. But we didn't have many, the Japanese preferring death to surrender, and so even though I was right behind the front lines I had time to play some catch with the Marines and even work up an exhibition game every now and then. That kept me busy and pleased the Marines. It was good to think about balls and strikes instead of the carnage that surrounded us.

After the armistice with Germany and the victory over the Japanese, I came home and took a job teaching Latin and Greek at Northwestern, and that teaching job left my summers free. I liked teaching, and I liked being a scholar; but I missed playing ball, and I come from a family that made its money in real estate, so I could spend money when I wanted. So I put together the Wandering Warriors, a name that I never explained to the others. We played in the Midwest Semipro League, from Davenport to Kankakee to Decatur to Carbondale to Paducah and then back up north to Crystal City and Hannibal and then Cedar Rapids and then over to Rockford. Round and round we traveled, staying on the circuit, playing one or two or three games in each town, and winding up having played sixty games before the summer came to an end.

There were just eleven of us and we knew we needed one more pitcher and a good utility infielder, but we hadn't found the right people for that yet. But we got by with eleven. I did the catching, and Quentin did the bulk of the pitching. He had a rubber arm, it seemed. Not much of a fastball, but a nice sinker and a good curveball and generally more junk than most hitters at this level could even imagine. Plus, he was a great guy and the closest thing I had to a best friend.

()

"How far, Quentin?" I asked him after some time.

"Another left," he said, "in about a mile. Ten miles on that, and we'll be there."

"Sure enough," I said, and slowed down some so we could see the road when we got to it. Which we did, but it wasn't much, just a dirt road with ruts. "You sure?"

"That's what the map shows," he said. He was using his Zippo to light up the map every now and again. That Zippo got him through some dark nights in Guadalcanal during the war, so I took that left.

It was slow going, maybe ten miles an hour, maybe less. I could have pointed out to Quentin that the more roundabout way on better roads would've gotten us there sooner; but he's our ace and he wins about all the time. His ball moves all over the place and he needs me back there behind the plate to catch that thing. And his curveball sometimes falls off the table and gets into the dirt, and he needs me for that too.

I was thinking about that, thinking about what a good battery we made, me and Quentin, positive and negative and all that, when the road went up a little rise, and when we crested that it dropped down steeply and there was a river, pretty good sized so maybe the Sangamon or the Mackinaw. And that was where the road stopped.

"Quentin?" I asked him.

"Oh, hell, Professor," he said, "this don't show on the map. I thought there'd be a bridge. Can we back our ass out of here?"

The mist was thicker near this water and getting thicker still. "We're here for the night, I think, Quentin," I said.

The guys were grumbling, wondering what the hell we'd gotten into. There were some pointed remarks as I opened the door and me and Quentin dug the flashlight out of the glove box and walked on down to the river. No bridge and never had been one, it looked like to me. But when Quentin shined his light across the river, we could see a good-sized ferry.

"You see that?" Quentin asked me.

"I do," I said, "but not for long in this damn river fog." And as I said that it disappeared into the darkness and the mist.

"Someone'll be there in the morning, I suspect," said Quentin.

I reached over to slap him on the back and say, "Heck, yes, Quentin, someone'll be there at first light, for sure, and we'll be at that old bandbox of a ballpark in Decatur not long after that. It'll all work out fine."

"I'm damn sorry, Professor," he said, but I told him not to worry, we'd get our sleep on the bus. Wouldn't be the first time or the last time we'd done that.

"Sure enough," he said, and we walked back with the bad news, told the guys how it was, and that we might as well get as comfortable as we could and try to get some sleep.

We were lucky the night was pretty cool. I took my duffel outside and sat on it, leaning back against a front tire. Quentin joined me and handed me his newspaper and his Zippo. I took a look at the headlines. Hitler's invasion of Spain and Portugal was going to end sometime soon with the fall of Lisbon. Part of the Armistice was that the exhausted Brits got to keep Gibraltar, so Hitler was about done for now, I figured. Maybe, in a year or two, he'd turn his attention again to England, but for now the Royal Navy and the overworked RAF would ensure the peace. And then there was Russia, still in turmoil after Stalin's assassination, but soon enough there'd be trouble there. Sure, we were at peace, but it wasn't going to last. At least we'd beaten the Japanese with that superbomb, and as long as we had that and the Germans and Russians didn't, we'd be okay. Fingers crossed. I wished freedom well, but I wasn't all that optimistic.

But here, now, in Illinois, we were a long way from being at war. Our only worry was getting some shut-eye in a bus by a sleepy summer river as the fog thickened. Tomorrow the Wandering Warriors came to town in Decatur, Illinois, for a three-game stint. We'd put on a show and maybe get ourselves back into first place if we won two out of the three. I figured we'd make about thirty dollars a man by way of pay. It wasn't much, but it kept us going.

I folded up the paper and set it on the ground. "We'll get 'em tomorrow," I said to Quentin.

"Sure we will," he said back. And then we both did our best to get comfortable. Quentin can sleep anywhere, but it took me a while and then, eventually, I drifted off.

2

QUENTIN

I was the last to wake, as always, but even before I woke up proper, I knew everything was wrong. I'd got chilled in the middle of the night and climbed up into the bus to stay warm. That seemed like a good idea at the time, but now the old Transit was swaying under me like I was all at sea, and I hadn't felt that way since those troop ships on the Pacific. I didn't like it then, and didn't now.

It was daylight and bright outside, but the wrong sort of bright, and I was all hot and sweaty, but it was somehow a different hot, with dusty smells in the air I couldn't place. I heard the Professor shouting, and he doesn't do that. He's a man who gets all quiet when he's angry and glares into your face instead of giving you what-for straight out.

Worst of all, I couldn't make out *what* he was shouting.

So I'm calling out, "All right!" and "What the heck now?" and getting to my feet and stumbling down the bus, which I'm alone on, bumping back and forth off the seat backs. The windows are damp with all our night sweat, and I'm peering and squinting and trying to make out who's who out there.

Then a blade flashed in the sunlight, and suddenly I was wideawake. I lunged for the nearest bag—Jimmy's, I think—and grabbed up a bat and jumped down the steps and out the front door of that bus real fast.

I expected good ol' boys, small-town know-nothings who don't take kindly to strangers camping by their land and even less kindly to folks of a darker hue such as myself and Walter. I had no doubts I'd be jumping into a fracas.

Was I expecting Romans, like from that Ben-Hur movie I snuck into as a little bitty kid? No. I was not.

Romans.

I stopped dead in my tracks and said a very bad word that I generally only whisper when I'm alone, in case the Lord gets angry.

Last night's fog had cleared. The river was still there, and the ferry, only now it was on this side of the river. But around us was no farmland, no corn, nothing but grass and olive trees, a whole orchard of them surrounding us. The dirt road under the bus led right to the water where that ferryboat had pulled up. It was short and wooden with low sides and places to tie off horses and a big oar at each end where the ferryman would stand and propel that thing. There'd been no Illinois ferry like that in a long time.

As for the sixteen Roman soldiers squaring off against the Professor and the others, they had helmets with plumes, and metal armor that covered their chests and arms in segments, and those odd kilty-skirty Roman things with the metal chains hanging down like an apron. Bare legs and leather sandals, and they all had short swords. Behind them stood a dozen folks egging on the soldiers, dressed in rough linen tunics, three of them carrying—I swear to God—pitchforks. Simple farm folk if I ever saw any, but not in shirts or denims or boots.

Six of those Roman soldiers had been pushing the bus around, trying to get it to move, I guess, and when they saw me come out the door of it they drew their swords and came at me.

I wondered for a second if we'd stumbled into some movie being made in the middle of Nowhere, Illinois, but then I heard the Professor standing up to them all with his head high and his chin thrust out, shouting in Latin, which I knew was Latin because he used it all the time to cuss at us when we needed it, and he liked to read to us sometimes from some book written by Julius Caesar himself way back a couple of thousand years ago, about battles with Vercingetorix and those wild Gauls and all.

The Roman with the sideways helmet plume who was shouting back in the same language looked strong and muscular, as if he could take any three of us down single-handed and then pitch a no-hitter right after with his other arm. And to be honest, our guys, standing behind the Professor, looked nine different kinds of terrified. The Wandering Warriors had wandered mighty far, and that was the truth.

That Roman who seemed in charge of things shouted at the six who were coming at me, and they stopped dead in their tracks. He barked another command, and in two seconds they were over with the others, so that the two sides, us and them, were now facing off twenty feet from the bus and nobody was even looking at me anymore. So when the Professor stepped forward, hands spread wide for calm and still spouting Latin, and the Roman leader upped and raised his sword high, there was no way my bat and me could get there in time to help. I'd been in hand-to-hand combat on Ie Shima so I mighta been useful too.

Instead, I jumped back up into the bus, put my hand on the ignition key, and turned it, and that engine started up with a loud backfire. The Professor had been working on the timing of that engine for a week now, and I was glad he hadn't been able to fix it.

That backfire cut through the babble of voices like all get-out. The Warriors all flinched like startled coneys, but they'd been hearing that backfire for days and weren't shook up by it. But the Romans, dear Lord, the Romans *threw* themselves back away from me and that old Ford Transit. The soldiers leaped, and the farm folk who had brought them ran, hands high and eyes rolling.

Well, I turned the engine off and stepped back outside the bus and said out loud, "Yes sirree, that is more like it. A little respect for the Professor. That is all we ask."

The Professor didn't even glance at me. He was still steel-eyeing that Roman in charge, trying to stare him down, intimidate him like he was the pitcher for a team we hated.

The Roman looked at me again, all uncertain, and at the bus, and lowered his sword. Then the two of them jabber-jawed away for what seemed like ten minutes, the Professor in his Julius Caesar Latin and the Roman in his rough, gritty version of the same. But they understood each other good enough, I could see that.

Then the Romans put their swords away and the Professor turned to the guys. "Get your stuff from the bus," he said. "Get your gloves and bats, bring the ball bag, all of that. And lock up behind you. We'll be taking a little walk with these boys to see what's what."

Jimmy shook his head, not understanding, on the verge of crying. "What about the game? The Dukes are expecting us. The game. This can't be happening!"

The Professor took a good look around, and down at the ground and up at the sky, and then he pinched his own arm so hard I could see the white mark.

Then he shook his head. "Jimmy," he said, "and you others, you all just keep it together and don't fret. I think we have a really, *really* long time ahead of us before that Decatur game begins."

"We're leaving the bus here?" asked young Davey.

The Professor wiped sweat from his forehead. "Best save the gas," is all he said.

We gathered up our things and started walking down to the river to the ferry. As we walked I looked at the guys, and it was sure that they didn't have a clue. They were all rattled and confused and scared, and probably not one in three with any idea how far we'd come, where we'd been brought to and why, and just how impossible this all was. Me, I believed the Professor had things in hand. Or I hoped so.

Romans beside and behind us, we went across on that ferry and then started walking, following a rough track between fields. I saw scrawny cows and a few pigs, real small. The Professor looked lost in thought, as if he was doing math. I didn't want to disturb those thoughts, but I just had to step up beside him.

"I'm sorry, Professor," I said.

"For what?" he said, irritated. "For firing up the bus and likely saving our lives?"

"Nope, for me gettin' us stranded here in God-knows-where-and-when."

He shook his head, and his voice softened. "You'll have to explain that to me, Quentin, because you have lost me and that's the truth."

"Because I was the one insisted we leave Route 66 behind and take them back roads," I said.

The Professor upped and laughed. It was the one moment in the whole adventure that I thought maybe he'd lost his marbles. It was a high, wild laugh and the Roman soldiers marching by our side and behind us clutched their sword hilts like they meant business.

"Hey, don't do that, Professor, you're making these guys nervous."

He said, "And to think that all morning I've been sure this all was *my* fault."

"And you figure that how?" I asked.

The Professor shrugged. "Maybe because we're in Ancient Rome and I speak Latin? That feels like we must be here because of me. But for my life I can't fathom why."

I nearly said to him, "You'll work it out, Professor." But I didn't, because that would've put all this on him and made him frown even harder.

14

So instead, I asked him, "Where are these Roman bruisers takin' us? What's next?"

About then we climbed to the top of that low ridge and there it was, a Roman road, right in front us, heading off both right and left. It was raised about a foot, had rocks along the sides and then smoothed out rocks on the top. It was about perfect to walk on.

We got up on there, and then the Professor looked over at me and said, "See that post over there, Quentin?"

I looked and I did see a post, a stone post maybe three feet tall, with some marks scratched into it.

"I do," I said. "What's it say?"

"That's called a millarium, Quentin, and the Romans used them to tell people how far it was to the next important place. A milestone."

"How far to what?" I asked.

"Unless I'm mistaken, Quentin, that sign means we're on the Appian Way, the most famous Roman road of them all. I'd say we're headed to Rome."

"Well, hell," I said, "I ain't never been to Rome, Professor." And he laughed. I added, "What are they going to do with us, do you think, when we get there?"

"Well, Quentin," he said, tugging up a bit on the duffel bag he was carrying that had all his catching gear, "I hope maybe we're going to play some ball."

I grinned at him. "Damnation, Professor, why didn't you tell us that a little sooner?"

3

THE PROFESSOR

The Appian Way! I knew the guys were terrified by all this, but for me it was all the excitement without—yet, anyway—any of the real danger. The Romans were calm, we weren't in slave chains, we were headed to Rome herself, and the centurion in charge seemed to have something definite in mind.

I had questions, a lot of them, like why was a centurion in charge of a dozen-plus soldiers and a few carts with civilian types walking along beside them. Centurions had eighty or a hundred legionaries under their command. And was it an accident they'd come across us in the morning? I'd asked the centurion that, and he'd just said he was under orders. His Latin and mine weren't quite on the same page, so I wasn't sure what he meant by that. But it was obvious that he wasn't all that surprised to find us, though the old Ford Transit's backfire had certainly shocked the hell out of the guy. I had to smile at that.

"What's so funny?" Quentin asked me. "You grinning about all this, Professor?"

I looked at him. My ace pitcher, a guy who'd fought at Iwo and Ie Shima and Saipan and was ready to land on Honshu when the bomb ended that war. A real hero. Amazing, really, that a guy like Quentin, sharp as a tack and a genuine war hero, couldn't stay at the team hotel in Paducah each time we went there. You had to wonder what he'd been fighting for.

"You daydreaming, Professor?" he was asking me.

I smiled again. "No," I said, "I was just thinking about you starting up the Transit, Quentin. These Romans about jumped out of those fancy uniforms."

"They sure enough did, Professor, but they don't seem too worried now. We're all marching along pretty good. And this duffel bag ain't all that good for carrying, you know?"

"I know." I shifted mine around some. "Let's try and keep up for another half hour or so and then I'll ask the centurion up there for a break, okay?"

Quentin nodded and then drifted back in line to tell the others, and I upped the pace a bit to catch up with the centurion. But it wasn't easy; he was used to moving along smartly, and I had my duffel slung over my shoulder. Plus, I had to admit, a lot of catching over the years had slowed me down. My knees didn't take nicely to all this walking. But I did get up there, finally, only to have his bodyguards cross their pila in front of me to make sure of my intentions. The centurion was up at the front, chatting with one of his officers as I got there, the two of them looking at something the centurion was holding.

I spoke up. "A word, please?"

He turned to look at me and frowned, waved the bodyguards off, and as I approached to within about ten feet of him, with not a bit of warning, he upped and threw what he was holding straight at my head.

I should've ducked or dodged it, but in that less-than-split-second, something clicked in my brain and I reached up with my left hand and caught it.

I wasn't wearing my catcher's mitt, of course. If it had been a rock with some edges on it, I might have wound up with a nasty cut. Instead, it just stung a bit. Like Quentin's fastball on a good day. Which made sense, since the thing he'd thrown at me was one of our baseballs. And the whole group of Romans marching along there laughed and nodded when I tossed it in the air and then lobbed it back to that centurion.

4

_____

QUENTIN

Well, that was it for hilarity. They waved the Professor back, and we never did get our break. If anything, they upped the pace. Some of our guys were panting, and even for me it was bringing back bad memories of the Marine Corps. As for the Professor, I could tell his legs were causing him trouble, though that frown on his face may not have been all about his knees.

And then the walls of Rome came in sight, and I could see the fear growing in the guys' eyes. They were muttering, looking around for a way out of this mess.

"Don't," I said in warning, "don't even give that a thought." And then I hustled up to walk next to the Professor. "Hey, me and the guys, we was wondering if this is really such a good idea."

"I'll talk to 'em," he said, and we both dropped back. "Fellows," he said, "You got to stay calm here, now, you hear me? No one makes a break for it, you hear? Don't make trouble, not now. You won't outrun these troops. We all stay together. This will be fine. We're a team. We came here together, and we'll leave together too." He gestured ahead of us and grinned. "Besides, we split up now, you guys'll miss out on the glory that's Rome."

"Heads down, now, guys," I added quietly. "Just you keep on

walking. Don't fret. Don't think too much. We'll get through this OK."

And so, not thinking too much, we walked through those massive gates and into the Eternal City.

Truth be told, I ... was expecting more. Streets paved with marble and gold, maybe. Grand men in togas and laurel wreaths striding the streets. Chariots? I'd seen those movies and listened to the Professor talk about Rome so much that the real thing was kind of a letdown at first.

Mostly, it looked dirty and poor. Grimy streets of rough stone, strewn with garbage and lined by high walls. Surly men in linen tunics and sandals. Clothes, knees, and faces filthy. The women looked unhappy and hard-bitten too. No one smiled— mostly they were watching the soldiers go by and looking worried about that.

Then the walls gave way to what looked like tenements, six stories high on either side of us, and right away the muck in the streets at our feet grew even worse. It smelled like bathrooms, and the end of the day at the market when the food is going rotten.

"Glory?" Danny Felton muttered rebelliously. Danny had a mouth on him, and we'd have to keep an eye on that. Good glove at third base, and a strong arm. But a short fuse. I shot him a look, but I knew what he meant. If Rome had any glory, it must be behind all those stout wooden doors that hid the homes away from the poor working stiffs.

The Professor was striding along in a trance, his face unread-able. I thought perhaps he hadn't heard Danny's sass. But then he nodded once and smiled thinly. "Just you wait a moment, oh Danny-boy. Glory's coming."

I started to feel my own fear squirming in my gut. I thought I was done with that, after surviving Iwo and Ie Shima and coming home in one piece. All I wanted to do after that was play some baseball, you know? I loved pitching, I loved being in control, painting some corners, moving somebody off the plate, keeping 'em guessing. And then your world turns upside down and you're walking along like it's just another day in ancient Rome and you realize that you never had any control at all in this world. You don't know anything. You're the one doing the guessing.

I wondered if maybe me and the Professor had been wrong after all. Perhaps we should've all made a big old break for it while we still had some countryside around us.

Then we took a right turn, and uh-oh. *Here* came the marble.

"What the—" said Danny, and I glared quickly at his profanity, but … oh Danny-boy.

5

THE PROFESSOR

I knew pretty much everything there was to know about the Colosseum, but in all the photographs it's two thousand years old and broken down, a heap of old stone that looks like it was sliced diagonally with a giant rusty gladius. Seeing it whole was mind-blowing. Curved walls a hundred fifty feet high lined with arches all around and all grand and golden and shiny and busy-looking.

And hell, Quentin and the guys recognized that thing straight off. I could feel their terror rise. My boys might not be all that well read, but every single one of them had heard of *gladiators*.

If the legionaries had tried to march us straight into that giant arena of stone and gold, the Warriors would have broken. I know it. All the discipline in the world couldn't have stopped some of them from bolting, and then the rest would've tried to follow. And God alone knows what would have happened next.

But they didn't. The centurion looked at me, and damn him, he *winked*, and then we turned and instead walked into the building next door, a low square functional-looking block with porticos across the front.

I heard Quentin murmuring calming things, and I could feel

everyone relax. Bobby Gamin, our left fielder, even cracked a funny about feasting and couches and such. I wasn't surprised, Bobby loved to go to the movies and I'm sure he'd seen *Quo Vadis* and *Ben-Hur* and plenty of Caesar and Cleopatra movies. The Claudette Colbert version of Cleo was a hoot, and the Vivien Leigh wasn't bad. Not accurate, I'd always thought, but not bad. It occurred to me that I was about to get a chance to see just how accurate all those movies and novels and history books had been.

Which wouldn't help me much if we all were dead. Unlike Bobby, I was far from relaxed.

No, we weren't going into the Colosseum. At least, not yet. Instead, Rome's soldier-boys were escorting us into the Ludus Magnus. Otherwise known as?

The Great Gladiatorial Training School.

And as we walked in the door, two legionaries grabbed my arms and half-lifted, half-dragged me away from my team.

Instant pandemonium. I heard Walter, our shortstop, shouting "Hey!", heard the other guys start to move, heard a fight breaking out behind me, and then the soldiers had me around the corner and bumping up the stairs before I could even call out and tell them to be calm, not to get themselves hurt.

6

THE PROFESSOR

I smelled her before I saw her. Oils and sweet unguents and rose water and maybe some powder. Either that, or Rome's Gladiatorial Training School kept a perfumery on the premises.

I'd stopped struggling two floors below; it would help nobody if I got myself killed or injured. Now the legionaries and I stood outside an open doorway with daylight and all those sweet aromas spilling out of it, so when the soldiers let me go, I smoothed down the ruffled clothes that I'd slept and hiked twenty miles in, in the vain hope of making myself a tiny bit presentable.

Then came a brisk command from inside the room in a low alto voice that was obviously used to being obeyed immediately. And, immediately, they marched me in.

To my right was a big open window that overlooked the circular courtyard in the center of the Ludus Magnus. There, a dozen groups of men battled with sword and shield, trident and net, whips, spears, and various other weapons. It looked like a giant brawl, but amid the grunts and the clamor of steel meeting steel, the voices that wafted up here to the third-floor overlook were focused, businesslike, even cheerful. This was not battle. This was practice.

But much as I wanted to look at the living history exhibit out in the training arena, I wanted to look at the noblewoman to my left even more.

The Romans I had seen so far had the olive skin common to many Italians. This woman's skin was two shades darker than that. Her hair was auburn, shoulder-length but coiffed into tight curls that hugged her head and looked as if they'd been arranged strand by strand. Perhaps they had; she was obviously rich enough to be able to spare the time.

Her eyes were large, penetrating, and rimmed with kohl. Her face was angular but beautiful. She looked commanding and confident, but I also saw something else in those eyes: an intense intelligence and curiosity. She looked about thirty years old.

I was willing to bet that the essences and fragrances her slaves had artfully applied to her hair and body today cost more than my whole team earned in a year. Do I need to add that she was dressed magnificently, in fine white linens hemmed with gold and silver threads, ornamented with what might have been gems?

I tore my eyes away. I was staring. And so I missed the gesture she must have made to the legionaries, because they saluted and withdrew, leaving us alone together.

Well, that was unexpected.

Under her stern gaze I did what anyone would have done, which was to drop my eyes, bow, and say a polite, "Good afternoon," to her in Latin.

She half-smiled, half-cringed, perhaps at my pronunciation. "Huh. So *you* are …"

And, just like that, she addressed me by name. My real name, not just Professor, which is what everyone calls me.

My mouth dropped open. No one on my team calls me by my real name. Hell, most of them don't even know it. She couldn't have heard it from any of the boys, even if she'd been with us.

My heart was hammering, fit to burst by now, but I tried to stay calm and merely nodded. "The same, ma'am." Then realized I'd stupidly said that in English, and in Latin repeated the sentiment: "Yes. That is my name."

Again, she cringed, but hey, she had a hell of an accent of her own. Far from schoolbook or church Latin, that was sure.

I bowed again. "And, please, what is yours?"

There must have been politer ways of asking, but I was lucky I could drag any Latin at all to mind at this precise moment.

"I am Domna," she said simply.

In Latin, *Domna* just means "Lady," so that was far from helpful. But I looked again and thought about it a trifle longer, and then said: "*Julia* Domna?"

Domna looked shocked, though whether at my knowledge or my over-familiarity wasn't clear. Then she inclined her head.

I smiled at her, and she shook her head slightly in amazement. I expect the people around her were trained not to meet her eye. I was not well-trained. "And, if you'll forgive me: how is your husband Septimius? And your sons?"

Now her face hardened and she looked as if she wanted to kill me. I backed off, literally; I stepped away three paces and lowered my gaze. "My apologies. *Many* apologies, Domna. I did not know. Severus is fallen?"

"He is," she said curtly and, turning her back, walked away from me.

Well. I hoped my clumsiness hadn't broken anything. But at least I now knew where—or *when*—we were.

The Colosseum was built and complete by 80 AD, so I'd known we were later than that. Styles of Roman dress had started changing in the fourth and fifth centuries, but that still gave me a wide window.

But if this was Julia Domna, and her husband Septimius Severus had died recently enough for her to be shocked at the mere mention of it, then this was 211 AD, or perhaps 212.

I fervently hoped it was 211. After old Septimius struck out, the next Emperor up to bat would be Caracalla, who was almost as nutty and violent as Caligula. If *he* was anywhere around here, we'd all have to be very careful indeed.

But then I remembered I had a much more bizarre problem at hand, because Julia Domna *knew who I was.*

"So it was you," I said to her back. "Julia Domna? You brought us here. Picked us up right out of time. Out of the years. To your year. To your place. To Rome."

It was the only way I could think to put it in Latin. But Domna did not respond, and so I stepped to the window and looked out at the gladiatorial practice. Trying to match her calmness, maintain some initiative.

Trying not to be desperately afraid that we would all end up down there or across the road in the Colosseum, me and Quentin and Walter and Enos and Jake and all the guys, with swords in our hands, swinging them like bats because that was what we knew, while brawny and utterly ruthless brutes like those in the courtyard below me rushed at us and hacked our lives away.

7

QUENTIN

The Romans stopped our little rebellion with an ease that bordered on contempt, and threw us into a pen. That's what I'd have to call it: a big square room, featureless in every way, just a few small windows up too high for any of us to see out of. They threw our bags in after us. At first, we just sat there, scared and angry. But time passed and nothing seemed to be going on, and then more time passed until Walter grabbed a ball and, still sitting down, started throwing it against a wall so it bounced back to him; just like you do when you're a kid. And then he stood up and started throwing it harder, so it came back on the short hop, which he backhanded and then flipped the ball into the air, caught it with his right hand and did it all over again.

Pretty soon Danny joined, and then so did I, and then Jake grabbed a bat and we started playing pepper and flipping the ball around like you do to each other, behind the back and all that, showing off for the fans. We had a good game, everybody loosening up and getting involved in one way or another. This was all weird as it could be; but, hell, we were ballplayers. It wasn't long before we were wisecracking, like you do, and flipping the ball all over the place. It took our minds off the trouble we were in.

And so, when the Professor came back to us, we looked like his Wandering Warriors, about ready to get out there and go nine against whatever them Romans had in mind.

He nodded briskly at us as if this wasn't the weirdest day of our entire lives and said, "Good. Let's go."

"Go?" said Davey.

"Go where?" I said with some suspicion.

The Professor shot me a look and said, "Outside, of course. To practice for real. As long as you boys promise to stop trying to fight everyone we see, that is."

We packed up and filed out. Playing a little pepper had lulled the fellas into some kind of normality in this crazy situation, and they all went meekly, trusting the Professor, but as we filed out of that pen he sidled up to me and, *sotto voce* as you might say, whispered, "Help me make this look good. We're playing for our lives here."

8

THE PROFESSOR

"All right, fellows," I told them, once we were out on the dirt and in the sunshine. "The Romans just want to see what baseball's all about, so I told them they could watch us work out."

It wasn't quite as simple as that, but I thought I'd better ease into it, so I was holding a ball in my right hand, tossing it up in the air and catching it while I talked. "These guys here are athletes, fellows, and they tell me they have a kid's game like baseball. They call it "small ball." So I told 'em we all started playing this game when we were kids too; but where we're from, adults play it, and it's pretty damn entertaining."

I tossed the ball toward Enos Slaughter, our center fielder and the fastest guy on the team. He'd steal second from his own mother if she looked the wrong way for a second or two, and he had a great glove and a strong arm out in center, as well. He and I usually warmed up together, and today was no different. He caught it, grinned, and threw it back to me.

And the guys knew what to do from there. Everybody broke into pairs and started playing catch, loosening up the arms and stretching out the muscles.

Then, just like a bunch of kids marking off a field when we

were ten-year-olds, we put down some caps to mark the bases. We had a rubber home plate with us, and we set that down for starters, and then used caps for first, second and third. Then I went over and found a couple of the rakes the Romans used to smooth out the dirt, and while the guys were loosening up I gave one of them to Bobby Gamin, and the two of us gave the infield the once-over. No grass and it wasn't pretty, but there weren't any rocks out there before and the dirt wasn't too bad. It was playable.

Normally we'd take batting practice then, and I always threw BP; but I was thinking maybe we'd dazzle those Romans a little bit first with some snazzy infield work, and let them see what outfield play is like too. So I had Quentin walk down the first base line with the fungo bat to hit some fly balls to the outfielders, and I used the other fungo to hit some grounders to the infielders.

Taking infield was always one of my favorite things to do, mainly because in some other life I'm a slick-fielding shortstop, backhanding that sharp grounder while I go toward third, and then pivoting on my right leg to bring my body around enough that I can sidearm the ball to first and beat the runner. So lots of times I'd get out there and trade off with Walter or Duke or Bobby and have some fun taking grounders.

But not here, not now. We needed to be at our entertaining best and that meant I was hitting the grounders and the guys were fielding them and looking sharp while they did it. I moved them around, hitting balls to their right or to their left, and hitting rollers or one-hoppers, and then a few infield pop flies. All so the guys could show off their skills. We did three rounds of throws to first, and then three more of turning two at second, and a few more turning two the hard way at first, and then a final round keeping Duke busy at third. Then I called in Quentin from hitting those fly balls and did my job as catcher while he dropped some bunts and then hit the ball to the outfield, and we made some plays at the plate. Our outfield arms were good, and the guys really showed that off. Quentin hit them fly balls they had to run to catch, but made sure they were playable. Then the guys set up the cut-offs and the Warriors were perfect as they threw to second and then to third and then to home. If you knew the game, it was a joy to see it played that well.

If you didn't know the game, I was sure hoping you'd appreciate what you were watching. Especially Domna. For all our sakes, I hoped to hell that she was up there in that room, looking out the window and liking what she was seeing.

After a half hour of that, I brought the infield in and told the guys it was time for batting practice. Then I grabbed the ball bag and walked out about sixty feet from our home plate and used the heel of the spikes to draw a line in the sand. That was my pitching rubber, and with Quentin wearing the tools of ignorance since we needed a backstop, I started throwing good fastballs right down the middle as the guys came up to take ten swings each. There was a guy at the plate, a guy on deck and another in the hole, and everyone else was shagging flies and grounders and tossing them back into me. As the hitters switched after their ten swings, I'd walk around and put all the balls that had rolled in back into the bag and we'd do the whole thing over again.

The right-handed hitters were having a field day. The way we had it set up, there was a short left field, no more than two hundred fifty feet, I'd guess. Then a good three-eighty or even four hundred to center, and forever, it seemed, off to right. The right-handed hitters were popping the ball over the fence with some regularity, and some of the legionaries and gladiators-in-training who were standing beyond the fence watching us got a chance to shag those balls and throw them back to us. That turned out to be a lot of fun, so much so that they started competing with each other to see who could make a nice bare-handed catch and then who had the best arm to throw it back onto the field. They were all a lot better at that than I'd thought they'd be.

Eventually all good things come to an end, and BP was over. Everybody'd had ten swings twice and most of the boys, even the lefties, had a homer or two to celebrate. I hit three of them out and laughed to think I'd probably ruined my nice level swing by trying for fly balls to left and batting-practice homers. But what the hell, we might not be alive long anyway, I might as well go out with some long balls. It felt good, even if it was a short left field.

○ ☽

I was the last to hit, so I was standing there with Quentin. He was still wearing the tools. The guys were trotting in from around the field. Looked like the workout was over. I wondered what was next? The only thing I was sure of was that it wouldn't be an afternoon game in Decatur, Illinois.

"Huh," said Quentin. "New player?"

I looked where he was looking, and there she was. Gone was the sumptuous dress; now she wore a plain grey tunic just like the rest of the Romans. Gone was the heavy waft of classical cosmetics, and her face was clean and shining and free of all makeup. A simple linen headband held her hair out of her eyes.

But more than her clothing had changed; it was her entire demeanor. For a woman—an empress of mighty Rome, for goodness sake—Julia Domna moved a lot like a ballplayer. Now that I knew she was mother to Caracalla and Geta, that meant she had to be mid to late thirties, but she sure as heck didn't look it.

She walked right up to us and said to me, in Latin. "I like your game. I played something very much like it when I was young. I was happy then."

Her words were flippant, even through that last part, but I saw a shadow move behind her eyes.

"Yes, Domna," I said to her. "Many of us play for similar reasons. Joy. Happiness. Childhood."

"Come then," she said, "and let us play." And she walked to her right, picked up Quentin's glove from where he'd dropped it, slid it onto her left hand, and said, "Give me a fastball, Professor, right down the middle."

Well, she'd picked that up by listening to us in batting practice, when the guys let me know what they wanted to hit. So I walked toward where we'd left our stuff and picked up my fielder's mitt and we got started playing some catch, me and the widow of the Emperor of all Rome, the mother of two sons contesting power, the focal point of a power struggle that would decide the fate of an empire and, maybe, the future of Western culture as well. Septimius Severus had managed to hold things together pretty good, but in the history I knew it was all downhill for Rome and the West from this point on. And here I was playing nice with Domna. I wondered, what the hell did she have in mind? Why were we here?

To play some ball, apparently. It turned out that Domna wasn't too bad. We played some catch and she loosened up, and then she trotted out to shortstop. Me and the guys all looked at one another and they shrugged. Hey, it was her home field. Walter and Bobby and Jake all trotted out to join her and then I hit her a soft grounder. Damned if she didn't charge the ball, gather it up pretty nicely, and then peg one over to Jake at first. Her arm motion was wrong, the sort of short-arm you see a lot in folks who learned the game late. She didn't bring the hand and wrist back far enough before firing it over to first.

But then I got a little more daring and hit one into the hole. She sprinted to her right, fielded it cleanly, and threw it sidearm to first. A rocket! "Good Christ Almighty," I heard Quentin say. He was next to me, catching up the balls as they came in from my odd new infield. "Did I just see what I just saw?"

I shook my head and laughed. "I saw it too, Quentin. She can play some ball."

"I'll be damned if she ain't a pretty good shortstop, Professor," he said, and then we watched as she went and proved that for another dozen or so ground balls. Sure, she was rough around the edges, throwing to the wrong side of the bag at second when she was trying to turn two. And she had trouble with pop-ups behind her. But, hell, who doesn't?

Most important, she was smiling, and having fun, and so were the guys. Sure, it was just one more strange thing in a long day of absurdities; but thank goodness she was as good as she was, since we were all still alive, even laughing and joking around, when she was done.

The guys had no idea who she was, which I figured was all to the good. If they thought she was just some rich wife of a Roman senator or something, that was fine with me.

I was about to try her out at bat when a bald man in a white tunic showed up in the entryway we'd all come in through and called out to her. I didn't catch what he said; by now I was so used to hearing Latin that by the time I realized he was speaking Greek, his words were scattered to the winds. Domna stopped where she was and turned, and a ball bounced past her into the infield.

Her expression had turned ominous. A quick nod to the messenger, another to me, and she was striding off the field with us all regretfully watching her go. Her body language had changed back again on a dime: imperious and commanding, she walked like a lady once more, not a ballplayer, for all that she was still wearing a tunic. At the edge of the field she remembered she was wearing Quentin's glove and dropped it into the dirt. Without even looking back she raised her hand in a curt signal to the stands, and then she was gone.

And as we all stood there, dumbfounded, the legionaries and gladiators who'd been our audience swarmed over the fence and came for us.

With cries of alarm the boys backed up, came together. Guys without bats snatched them from the ground. I heard Quentin saying, "Hey now, hey now," trying to calm them and Danny Felton saying, "Not that jail cell again, no way," and my other boys saying viler things in their fear as those brutes marched towards us.

I took a deep breath, smiled, and stepped forward.

( )

That night, I dined with an empress.

If I lived in Rome for a hundred years, I don't think I'd ever get used to eating lying down. I managed it for the first course of oysters, eggs, and turtle dove, but when they brought in the roast boar and poached lamprey, I begged and bowed and scraped and with a thousand pardons to my hostess, swung my legs off the couch and sat upright like a barbarian, stifling a belch. Wasn't sure I could eat a whole lot more of that rich food, anyway. I don't know how Domna could stay so slim on such a diet, and I felt bad for my boys, who were still back in the Ludus Magnus eating whatever the gladiators ate.

At least they wouldn't be herded back into the pen later. Tonight, my Warriors would be sleeping in the cells the most favored gladiators got, two men to a room, with a straw mattress each and a window for light and air. It wasn't luxury, but it wasn't a whole lot worse than some of the motels we stayed at on the road and was even a step up from sleeping on the bus. And they wouldn't be locked in. They couldn't leave the Ludus Magnus, but they were free to wander the halls, go to the latrines, or visit with one another.

Not that they'd be socializing a whole lot. They were dog tired. Turned out that those tough-as-nails legionaries and the even more terrifying gladiators, with all their brawn and scars and deadly swagger, all they wanted was to try their hand with a bat and ball. We'd had ourselves a four-hour pickup game, splitting into groups and trying to train the Romans up, show them what was what on a ballfield.

Not a one had Domna's skills, or anywhere close to that, but they had strong arms and dexterity and a ton of stamina. They were relentless, in fact. Either baseball had really stirred something within the savage breast, or they wanted to excel to curry favor with Domna. Either way, by the end we had to beg for mercy and it was only dusk that saved us.

I'd already known that the Romans played something like baseball, using a stitched-leather ball just a little bigger than a baseball, smaller than those used in their other ball sports. Roman women played it too, but their version had a lot fewer collisions and relied on finesse where the men relied on contact. But in both cases the players threw the ball, caught it, and even hit it, with sticks not that far different from baseball bats.

And as I was learning from Domna at dinner, her sons Antoninus—whom history would remember as Caracalla—and Geta also played the game and loved it.

Domna's late husband had been off fighting a war in Caledonia with both his sons when he had taken ill and died. The history I remembered said that it might have been poison. The boys had wrapped up the military campaign in short order, and were now marching their armies back to the Eternal City.

"And so, they come," she said. "Quarrelling all the way. Sometimes coming to blows, held apart only by their legates and tribunes. They are talking of splitting the body in two."

I shook my head, aghast. "Not ... forgive me, Domna ... you speak of the Emperor's body? Surely you do not."

Like the Brits and the Americans back home, Julia Domna and I were divided by a common language. I understood her words well enough but her idiom could be impenetrable, and to make it worse she was speaking Greek now. Turns out that Latin was her fourth language, after Punic, Aramaic, and Greek, which at least explained her accent.

Mercifully, she looked amused at my error of understanding.

Domna raised a finger, and a slave hurried to spoon more fish onto her plate and fill up her beaker of wine and water. She switched to Latin. "I speak of the Imperium, Magister. They would divide my husband's empire, and rule half of it each. But that cannot stand."

I wasn't sure I liked "*magister*," but there were worse things she could have called me. "And so, small ball."

She was staring beyond me now, into the shadows behind the oil lamps that lined the walls, or perhaps even further back into the past. "My boys. When young, they played all the time. Competing, always, but laughing all the while. And then they grew up." She sighed. "These past years, it was only Severus who stopped them from killing each other."

Best to check, even though I thought I understood. "But now …?"

"But now, during the great Games that will begin as soon as my sons return, Rome will play ball. And perhaps my boys will relax and be calm once more, and even laugh, and there will be peace between them."

Maybe I could take advantage of her reverie. I sat forward. "And so you chose us. But how on earth did you bring us here?"

Her gaze swiveled back to me, and she smiled enigmatically. "By the grace of the True God."

I considered that. "Which God?"

No God I knew, as it turned out. She spoke of Elagabal, the god of her homeland. Julia Domna was descended from a ruling dynasty of Priest-Kings in Syria, and her father was the High Priest of the Temple of the Sun God there, and so Domna had herself some serious favor with Elagabal. The True God spoke to her. She heard him, and she talked right back at him. Elagabal had told Julia Domna how to summon some entertaining warriors for the Games in the Colosseum marking Geta's and Caracalla's return, and even told her where to send the centurion and his guards to find us.

I frankly didn't know what to think about this ancient-world scripturizing and magicking, but Julia seemed sane enough to me, and we were all here now, and that was indisputable.

And perhaps the real story didn't matter. Somebody—or something, somewhere—had done an amazing thing, and that was probably about all I was ever going to find out about the mechanism of it.

I nodded diffidently, and with my heart in my mouth but as much confidence as I could muster, I said: "And when I and my Wandering Warriors have entertained you and Rome, and once your sons are reconciled? By the grace of the True God and yourself, we may return home?"

Again, that beautiful but Sphinx-like grin. "If Elagabal wills it," she said. And that was all I got out of her on that subject.

Using a traveling ball team from the future to heal a horrendous broken family and hold an empire together seemed like a tall order. I raised my own cup to my lips, and then put it down again. No more wine for me tonight. I needed to think.

"If your ... boys play anywhere near as well as you do, it will be a great game," I said. With Caracalla's fearsome reputation, it was hard for me to keep calling him a mere boy, like a mother would.

Julia Domna shrugged. "They are not bad. They move quickly, think on their feet. Catch and throw the small ball well."

I nodded. "And today, while we were playing, your slave came to tell you ... what?"

She brought those beautiful eyes to bear on me again, and studied me intently. I very nearly blushed. Maybe I even did. All I know is that I tried my best to withstand that gaze while she decided whether to tell me.

Eventually she said, "That 'slave' is a freedman. And word travels slowly on the road, and armies ride fast when they are angry."

"Yes, indeed," I said expectantly, but she had lapsed back into brooding, so I had to figure it out for myself. "Domna, when do Caracalla and Geta arrive back in the City? Perhaps sooner than you expected?"

"I had thought we had two months to train," she said. "Yet we have only one. Perhaps even less than that."

I whistled. "Then I hope your legionaries and gladiators learn fast."

Domna inclined her head. "With such a magister to teach them, I'm sure they will. But I grow tired of your many questions. Tell me more of ... where you come from. Of your time, and the game, and where you play it? There is much that I would know of you and your home year, Magister."

I hesitated for a long moment, even beckoning for yet another plate of food to give me time to think. But I couldn't cotton to a single reason to stay silent. Would telling Julia Domna about the twentieth century alter the future? Surely nowhere near as much as having my boys and me sliding back in time.

And if nothing else, I needed the grace and favor of Julia Domna, the absolute ruler of the Roman Empire ... at least, until her dangerous, violent sons came home.

And perhaps it wouldn't hurt to take my own mind off the seriousness of our situation, and brag just a little to a beautiful woman.

So, sure. I started telling her some baseball stories. About how Wally Pipp played through pain to become one of the Yankees' greatest first basemen, and how Babe Ruth won three hundred career games pitching for the Red Sox, and how Ted Williams was one of the greatest hitters of all time until he got shot down over China when MacArthur crossed the Yalu River in the China War. I told her how baseball was so much a part of life where we came from that we used its terminology all the time, hitting a homer with a new proposal at the office, or striking out if the boss said no. Or touching base with someone if you just wanted to check in with them on something. Or surprising someone during a meeting by throwing them a curve.

Or stepping up to the plate if you were going to take responsibility for something.

She laughed, and I hadn't seen her do that before. "But that's what you and I are doing here, Magister. We are stepping up to the plate, yes?"

"Yes," I said. "That's about it." And, I thought but didn't say, this might work out, even though the whole crazy thing was definitely out of left field.

( )

Two weeks later, I crouched behind the plate while Lucius Aurelius, the centurion who'd been sent to fetch us from the banks of the Tiber, delivered a pretty good curveball to me. Sure, he liked the high, hard fastball the best and I couldn't blame him. He was a soldier and in line for the Praetorian Guard. He didn't like to nibble at the corners. Straight heat, that was him, and I was having a hard time convincing him otherwise. But his curveball curved, so I was proud of him. And he had the knack of good control. Control is mostly a matter of belief on the part of a pitcher. You can't aim the ball when you let go, you have to just know that the motion you're using and the release point that feels natural will result in the ball going where you want it to. It takes a lot of confidence, and Lucius had that in spades.

We had four full teams now, all told: the Wandering Warriors, plus three squads of Romans. Eventually there would be seven Roman teams, one named for each of the hills of Rome, but for the time being, we just had the Palatines, the Aventines, and the Caelians. Today we were practicing all mixed up with the Palatines, who were Praetorians and other favored soldiers. They were okay; strong, disciplined, probably the most skilled, but taking time to gel as a team. The Caelians were a bunch of cheerful duffers, citizens of Rome who had started coming to the public practices out of curiosity and signed up to try the game for themselves. They worked great as a team, but most had no real ball skills. The Aventines were terrifying: gladiators all, they played with brute force and a lack of subtlety and would occasionally thump us or start fights when we got them out.

For the time being, we were playing here and there in the minor arenas around the city and even outside, building up support and interest. We would play our full-up showcase games in front of the co-emperors Caracalla and Geta, maybe a week or two from now. Perhaps even with them playing on the teams, if they wanted to step up to the plate. Domna would be playing with the Warriors and we were glad to have her. That meant moving Walter out of short and putting him in right field, or using him to pinch-hit and pinch-run, but he was okay with that.

She seemed to get better every day on defense. Good glove, soft hands, strong arm, turned the corner great in a double play. She had a flat swing and not much power at the plate, but as a singles hitter, she could spray the ball around and move the runners, and we needed that. Plus, we had to be careful with her, but it was fun to listen to her from the bench yelling at us to just get the bat on the ball, or hit it outa here.

Those showcase games would be played in the Colosseum, in between gladiatorial bouts. It would take some work to get the field ready for baseball after the gladiators had at it and there was blood on the dirt and sand; but the Romans could work miracles with that place, I'm telling you. They showed me how they could stage a sea battle in there, water and all, when they wanted to. I believed them.

I was enjoying the neighborhood games. Not too many spectators, but those who showed up seemed to be sticking around, figuring out how the game worked, enjoying the sportsmanship, applauding some nice work with the glove or a line drive in the gap, and then cheering with gusto for home runs. But the thought of playing in front of a bloodthirsty Colosseum crowd chilled me to the bone.

Nothing I could do about that, of course. Domna's city, Domna's rules.

Every day, the armies of the two brothers got closer. And every day I could feel the tensions rising on the streets of Rome.

I talked with Julia Domna most every day now. She was fascinated by us and keenly interested in the land we came from, far away in time: Land of the Free, Home of the Brave, a country of cars and airplanes and other marvels, of education for all, of sports stadiums where massive death wasn't part of the program. Every day she had new questions, and some of them were really *good* questions that I couldn't answer.

But if I had to eat much more peacock and lamprey and dormouse, my innards were going to revolt. So whenever I saw Domna's freedman standing in the archway to the Ludus Magnus arena, my heart sank a bit. Julia, she was good company, but frankly I'd rather have eaten the gruel and plain boiled meat my boys got.

And I'd rather have stayed with the boys for other reasons too. I saw the looks as I walked away from home plate, unclipping my shin guards and chest protector and handing my catcher's mask and mitt to Quentin. I'd rather be with them, building the team, than have them jealous and muttering behind my back.

But Julia Domna was the boss around here, and if we were ever going home, I'd be doing whatever she said.

()

I didn't like going to the Palatine Hill after dark to dine with Domna. I'd be ushered through stinking streets by lantern light, grateful for the escort of the soldiers. The only other men abroad by night slunk in the shadows, mean and vicious-looking, or were carried by in sedan chairs with their own toughs to guard them. On my own and unprotected, I'd not have lasted five minutes.

Today, though, it was still late afternoon, and the streets were bustling with men and women, citizens and slaves alike, all hurrying back to wherever they were going to spend the night, or grabbing a bite in the tiny bars and taverns that seemed to line every street. It wasn't all Latin I heard on those streets, either; Romans mixed with folks speaking Germanic, Gallic, Greek, Hebrew, and several African tongues. Rome of this era was truly cosmopolitan, and as best I could see no one was being turned away from the pie shops and wine stalls because of creed or color. It looked like Jake and I and the "Cubans" might actually be treated more decently here than at home, which gave me pause, I have to say.

But much as I'd have longed to linger and explore, my soldiers hurried me through the streets and into a tunnel and up some stairs, and before I knew it I was in the palace of Julia Domna once again.

I thought I'd been dreading dinner, but I'd been using that word all wrong. Because Domna's freedman led me into a room I'd never been in before, and all of a sudden four tough-looking legionaries I didn't recognize appeared from nowhere.

They kicked my legs out from under me so I fell onto my knees, further pushing my head forward into a kowtow while roughly holding my hands behind my back.

With good old American oaths on my lips due to the pain in my legs, I looked up.

He was a bulldog of a man, his face square and flat and pugnacious, his hair cropped brutally short and his beard barely more than stubble. He walked toward me with his head forward, seeming to lead with his brow. He looked like a man afraid of nothing. No, that's not right: he looked like a man much more used to inspiring fear than feeling it himself.

Caracalla. And Julia Domna was nowhere in sight.

Okay, so *this* was what dread really felt like.

"Good evening, Imperial Majesty," I began in Latin, in the

politest and most deferential tone I could manage. "My name is—"

Caracalla leaped forward and kicked me in the guts, hard. Knocked the wind right out of me. The soldiers dropped me to the floor, and so I did about the only thing I could think of, which was to curl up into a ball and protect my head when they started kicking me some more.

9

QUENTIN

Well, it was a shame that the Professor was called away, because the Wandering Warriors found ourselves visited by royalty, or whatever they call it when it's emperors and not kings.

We'd finished up our practice and were getting some chow, the usual gruel, more like breakfast porridge or grits than what a man would like for dinner; but tonight they brought us some salted ham and some olives and wine to go along with it. This cheered the boys up some, but not a lot, because they never liked it when we were separated from the Professor. We ate in the same long, low hall as the gladiators, but they mostly sat on their own benches to eat and didn't mix with us, which was fine. Those brutes scared the tar out of us.

So the fellas were grousing, but not too loud, while stuffing their faces, and then a tall and aristocratic young man walked in with an even taller Praetorian Guard on either side of him, and all the gladiators jumped and fell right down onto the floor and pressed their foreheads into the floorboards, and that was how we met the Co-Emperor, Geta.

Of course, without the Professor, conversation was all but impossible. None of us spoke Geta's languages—he tried several —and we tried what few we knew: a little Spanish, a little Italian, and some Yiddish. But he smiled and clasped every one of us by the arm and studied us and mimed throwing and catching a ball, and gave us to believe by signs that he would be coming back to see us in daytime and actually play a bit. Walter and Davey were all for getting a ball now and trying to get some catch going once they realized he was an Emperor and all—even they could understand we needed to impress the powers-that-be, whenever possible—but Geta obviously had somewhere else to be, and after smiling a bit more, he left.

Wow. An Emperor. That bucked up the boys and no mistake, and made those gladiators look at us with a bit more respect as well, given that he'd spent twenty minutes trying to talk to us and had ignored them completely. So after Geta left the guys all went back for more food, even though the ham was all gone and it was just gruel again now, and another cup of wine, and the mood in the room got about as downright cheerful and neighborly as it had gotten since we had arrived in this time and place.

And I sat back and thought, well now, maybe everything's going to be all right after all.

10

THE PROFESSOR

They dragged me along the corridor by my arms. Apparently walking under my own steam wasn't allowed, and I frankly didn't have my breath back anyway.

My ribs still ached, but I didn't think these goons had broken any.

Now a familiar voice, shouting. Julia Domna was marching down the corridor in her full makeup and hair, jewels dripping over a dress of white and purple, her expression livid. She walked right up to her son and got in his face, and he shouted back and pushed at her shoulder, and she shoved back. Caracalla was bellowing now, almost spitting, his face red and apoplectic. I couldn't understand a single word; they must have been speaking one of their other languages, Punic or Aramaic or whatever.

For all that Caracalla was a young guy—barely into his twenties, my guess—I found myself harboring the unworthy hope he'd just have a heart attack and die right there.

His soldiers had dropped back and were watching, hands on their gladius hilts, which scared me. Would Caracalla order them to draw steel on his own mother?

Almost as bad. She raised her arms above her head, almost as if she was going to pitch a spell on him, and at that Caracalla stepped up and punched her full in the face. Domna went over backwards.

I howled and tried to struggle up but Caracalla's legionary put his foot on my shoulder and trod me back down to the floor, and there I lay until Caracalla and his bully boys swept out, leaving me and the Empress Julia Domna sprawled on the marble floor, gasping like fishes. We weren't in great shape, either of us; but at least they'd left us alive. I had Domna to thank for that.

11

QUENTIN

The warm glow had worn off by bedtime, because the Professor hadn't come back. Most of the boys took it okay, heading off to their cells without mentioning it. But Danny Felton had a face on him like thunder, and he kept checking his wristwatch; and Enos, always impatient, was pacing.

Eventually I made 'em go to bed, trying to sound as calm and confident as I could, and I toddled off to my own cell too, where I lay on my back and stared at the ceiling for a long while.

I mean, I knew the Professor was having dinner with a pretty woman and all, but somehow, I just didn't see him abandoning us to stay out for a night on the tiles with Julia Domna. I didn't see that at all.

1 2

THE PROFESSOR

We sat there, side by side in the corridor on the hard marble floor, our backs against a sumptuous fresco of the procession of Dionysus. Julia hugged her knees and rocked, lost in her thoughts, and I gave her a moment. She didn't suggest going anywhere else, and so I didn't either. Perhaps moving would have made it more likely we'd run into her psychopathic son again.

"He is much worse," she said, almost to herself. "Maybe it was all the war, all the fighting. Maybe the death of his father. Some demon has him."

Or maybe, I thought, Caracalla just thought this was how you had to behave to be an emperor. If I remembered my history right, Septimius Severus had been no angel either, especially when he was young. But I said nothing.

Julia peered at me. "Understand, I have not seen him for three years, since he and my husband left to campaign in Caledonia. I had thought he would learn from his father, gain a cool head, grow out of his ... rages. But ..." She shook her head. "Whatever happens, do not address him unless you absolutely must. Never argue. Never answer back. He will find any excuse to throw you to the lions, or just slit your throat and be done with it."

I shivered. "All right. But what did he say to you?"

Domna blew out a breath, exercised her jaw back and forth. She was going to have a lovely bruise. "He is the Emperor, and he is very angry with me. And I am nothing. He made it very clear that he can have me killed whenever he likes. He wanted to remind me of that." She looked at me again with those piercing eyes. "And if he does kill me, you must do whatever you can to get away, because you will be next."

I nodded. No surprises yet. "But what's he got to be so mad about? I mean today, specifically?"

Domna looked desolate. "I was not expecting my sons for another week or more. But they galloped ahead of their armies with just a few centuries of men to protect them, because they had heard rumors from Rome. About you. Together, they burst in on me, at noon."

She checked the corridor. No one else about, so she reached out a pretty, long-fingered hand and wrapped it around mine. I squeezed her hand, and she looked down in surprise and then up at me again. "It is really my fault. I made a promise. The deep magics of Elagabal, I swore I'd only use by the grace of Septimius. And I have not, not until he died. But Caracalla says that now that I should only use them by *his* grace, when he gives his blessing. And he did not bless …" She gestured. "This. You."

"He's afraid of you."

She looked dark. "Maybe he should be."

I thought about it some more. "How about Geta? They're co-emperors, right?"

"Geta is a much nicer man. Calmer. A better son. And no match for his brother."

"So where is Geta now?"

"Probably barricaded into his own wing of the palace, behind his guards, so that Caracalla won't slay him in the night."

This was terrible. My mouth was dry, but I had to know. "Are we dead, Julia? Me and my boys? Is this over?"

"Not yet. Because the streets are buzzing about you and the

Wanderers. Caracalla cannot just make you disappear before the Games." She grinned wryly, still wincing at the pain in her jaw. "There was method in my madness. Robbing the people of their bread and circuses would be an unpopular move. And above all else, my son craves the popularity of the plebs. So he will have to find another excuse."

"We can't ..." I shook my head, thinking of Quentin and Davey, Danny and Walter and Enos and Jake and all, waiting patiently over in the Ludus Magnus like lambs before the slaughter.

And so I turned to her properly, and seized her arms and looked into her eyes. "Send us back, Julia. You magicked us here, you and the god Elagabal. Magic us away again. They don't deserve to be embroiled in all this, my boys; they're young and they're good kids and they just want to play ball. Damn it, you've been on the team for weeks, you know them, and not a one of them has a savage bone in his body. We're not just your toys, to perform and get slaughtered if it doesn't work out. Send us back home. Please."

Julia was already shaking her head. Gently, she pulled her arms away but rested her hand against my cheek. "I wish I could, Magister. But for that, you would all have to be out of the city. Rome is protected against the spells of foreign gods. We would need to get you far away. And that is not possible now."

I pushed her hand away. "Well, then, I should get home. Back to the Ludus Magnus, I mean, to tell my boys what's up."

Again, Julia shook her head. "The Palace is locked down for the night, and now that Caracalla is back, the Praetorians answer to him. I cannot order them out to guard you. You will need to stay here until morning."

My eyes swiveled to look into hers, incredulous. Surely she didn't mean ...?

No, she didn't. She poked my arm and grinned, a little ruefully. "No. Not that. But it will be a long night. Because we need to make a plan, you and I. Perhaps several plans."

You might at least say you're sorry, I thought, but now wasn't the time. And this wasn't even all about us; the Dowager Empress Julia Domna was in some pretty terrific danger herself.

If she wanted my help to plan and scheme our way out of this mess, then sure, I'd take her up on that. "All right. But are there any of those couches nearby?"

I pushed myself off the cold hard floor and up onto my feet, and reached a hand down to pull her up with me.

13

QUENTIN

"Where's the Professor? *Ubi est Magister?*"

The master of the Ludus—*lanista*, in Latin—stood with his arms folded and three toughs behind him covered in oil and muscle. I tried again. "We don't go out there and practice, we don't do anything, till we see the Professor again." I mimed it. Pointed outside, then crossed it out in the air with two decisive sweeps of my finger and folded my own arms. "Professor. Magister. Bring him back."

Behind me I heard Jimmy mutter a prayer and felt, rather than saw, Johnny Holman elbow him to make him shut up.

Morning light streamed through the high windows. We all could hear the gladiators already at work outside, whacking at one another with swords and tridents. The hard work of the day was beginning in the Ludus Magnus, and still we had no Professor.

We were all terrified; me too, but we had to make a stand.

The lanista pointed outside, mimed a bat swing and a catch. He was getting mad at us, and he was a man used to putting down trouble. I could see his toughs glaring at us, bouncing on the balls of their feet, ready to beat the living heck out of us.

There was a knock on the big doors, down the corridor, and

ALAN SMALE AND RICK WILBER

everyone looked that way. The door-boys cranked the doors, the
guards snapped to attention.

In walked the Emperor Geta, in a simple tunic, dressed for
ball, with a few soldiers behind him.

Everyone's face fell, because we'd been hoping for the Professor. I stepped up to Geta. "Professor? Magister?" I even used his
real name, and then raised my hands. "Where? *Ubi est Magister?*"

He obviously didn't know. And, equally obviously, had come
to practice with us.

I hesitated.

"I don't care who he is, we still don't go out there till we get
the Professor back." Danny Felton said. Of course it'd be Danny,
the only Warrior who would actually start a bar fight.

But the others were stepping away, lowering their bats.
"C'mon, he's the Emperor," said Walter. "We cross the Emperor,
we're toast. There's dumb, and then there's *stupid.*"

"*Co*-Emperor," Danny muttered, but Walter was right. We
weren't about to go on strike with royalty standing there.

So we got changed, and we went out to play some ball.

14

THE PROFESSOR

The next morning, I stood in the Roman Forum and did a long slow scan around it, still scarcely believing what I was seeing. Marble buildings surrounded me. Right next to me stood a huge triumphal arch. To my immediate left was the Curia, the Roman Senate House. Extending in front of me to my left was the civil Basilica of Aemilius and facing it to my right was another glorious-looking public building, the Basilica of Julius, all marble pillars and statues and spires. Arrayed behind me were temples to Vespasian and Saturn; across the Forum in front of me were temples to the deified Julius Caesar, and to Castor and Pollux, and between and beyond them I could glimpse the one that out-templed them all, the grand Temple of the Vestal Virgins.

And all around us a throng of people, hustle and bustle, the highborn and low, plus a few in legionary gear. Occasionally a sedan chair would nose through, held up by six brawny slaves; or patricians in togas would hurry by with their bodyguards, who could easily have been ex-gladiators by their bulk and scars. But by and large these were ordinary townsfolk in their plain tunics or rags, milling through and around the great Forum Romanorum and giving not a second glance to the opulence that surrounded them.

So this was Ancient Rome ... except that it wasn't ancient yet. The Arch of Septimius Severus at my shoulder was less than ten years old, built in 203 AD. Some of the other buildings and monuments around me must have been a hundred years old, or even two, but they were built stout and firm of good rock and marble and looked like they'd survive, well, a couple thousand years easily.

This was a living, breathing city of a million people. The greatest city in the world. I could have touristed it for a month, but I had only hours. I had work to do. And the Games to prepare for. Because over and above the temples I could see the line of the Colosseum, brooding over the city like a curse.

The Wandering Warriors would be in there very soon, in the arena, playing to a crowd that was more used to blood than ball games, our lives at the disposal of a capricious and psychopathic Emperor.

But still ... Rome was damned beautiful. Just standing here was a dream come true.

I cleared my throat to try to shift the lump in it, shook my head, and turned to Lucius Aurelius and the two squaddies who stood behind him. My own bodyguards, courtesy of Julia Domna, to make sure I didn't get myself killed in the streets or try to do a runner. Not that I had anywhere I could go, and not that I would ever have left my team behind.

"All right," I said. "Next I need to see the Sacra Via and then whatever the road is that leads to the east of the Palatine, and then we can take a look in at the Colosseum."

Lucius damn near saluted before he remembered he was in a plain tunic today, all of us incognito. He just nodded, and I grinned at him, and off we went.

15

QUENTIN

We were missing two good players, Domna and the Professor, but when an emperor wants to practice, you practice. So we worked out Geta pretty hard.

He was a banjo hitter, but like his mother he had good, soft hands, so when we took infield, we tried him out at third, short, and second. It turned out he didn't have his mother's strong arm, so without making any kind of fuss over it—the last thing we wanted to do was cause a ruckus with a co-emperor—we left him at second once he got there.

It was hard to figure where he got the necessary skills to get those short hops, but get 'em he did. And he moved side-to-side real smooth, so on routine grounders anywhere near him, he was fine. When he had to go deep up the middle and backhand the ball, he was okay getting his glove on it, but he just didn't have the arm to get the ball to first. It was all he could do to spin on that right foot and try to sling it in the right direction.

We worked him hard, sure, but he seemed to be having a good time. A great time, in fact. When he booted a grounder, he laughed about it and waved at me to hit him another one. When he took batting practice, he slapped at it, but darned if he didn't hit enough bloopers that you'd think he'd get some base hits, and he really sprayed the ball around.

Really, the guys were impressed, and so was I. And working him out gave us a chance to work out ourselves one more time before the Games, so we took it seriously. There was a lot riding on how we did on the field against these Romans.

Working him out also gave us a chance to focus on something other than the missing Professor. But as soon as I picked up the fungo to hit infield, I was reminded that the heart and soul of the Wandering Warriors wasn't here. He'd normally be hitting infield while I hit fly balls to the outfielders, but we couldn't do it that way and it worried the hell out of me. Where was he? Would he get back to us in time for the first game? It was mid-morning now and the first game was set for noon, the Warriors against the Caelians. It should be a laugher, but it was one we couldn't afford to lose. Without the Professor or Domna, we didn't want to take the Caelians too lightly.

All too soon, and before I was really ready, it was time to go. The lanista blew a whistle to get us all to line up, and some of the gladiators came over to punch our shoulders and grasp our forearms in that Roman way of shaking hands. Others looked sour at us, maybe because they'd be fighting to the death today and we'd just be batting a ball around.

At least, I sure *hoped* we weren't about to be in any kind of real combat. But who the heck really knew? We were in *Rome*. I had the feeling anything could turn into a blood sport here, at the drop of a hat.

Even without us, the Games were already heating up. We'd heard the noise of the crowds in the plaza outside the Ludus Magnus since early morning, and now that was being drowned out by a steadily growing din from inside the Colosseum itself, just beyond. Excitement was building. Excitement for the Games.

I had a dull ache in my belly, the acid taste of fear. I didn't want to do this. Wanted to be far away. In distance, and especially in years. I played baseball for fun, you know? I'd had plenty of fear during the war and I didn't want any more of it. But hell, we had no choice. It was time to go play ball.

16

THE PROFESSOR

After I'd scoped out the city, I went with Lucius to watch the Wandering Warriors play the Caelians in the first game. This was one I was sure the guys could win without me, so I wasn't worried about not being with them. Yet.

It was amazing just being there. The Amphitheatrum Flavium, on the first day of the Games in Memory of the Emperor Septimius Severus, and in Commemoration of His Great Victories in Caledonia.

The Emperor is dead, long live the Emperors. Hmm.

I came in just like any other paying customer, past the hundred-foot-high gilded statue of the long-dead Nero in the plaza outside and in through one of the sixty-six vaulted entranceways that ringed the place. I liked to get the feel of a ballpark before a game, to absorb the atmosphere of the place through my skin, and today was no different. But the ballparks I knew weren't this solid. The Colosseum was mostly limestone, with lateral walls inside of brick, concrete, volcanic tufa, and pumice. With Lucius by my side, I climbed up stone stairs surrounded by excited crowds and the reeks of sweat and cooked meat and spice and stale beer.

I came back out into daylight in the third tier of seats, over a

62

hundred feet above the level of the arena, and looked around me.

At once, I took in the arrangement; the Emperor's box at the north end, where Caracalla and Domna now sat, the Vestal Virgins' box across at the south end facing it. All around the arena at the same level were the expensive seats for the senatorial class. The next tier up was for nobles, and above them, where I stood, was the area reserved for the ordinary people of Rome. Stretching above and behind me were the seats for the women and the poor. There, the seats were of wood rather than the stone of the lower levels. It looked steep, rickety, and dangerous, a death trap waiting to happen. At every level the tiers were divided into sections, and most of those sections were already packed with citizens of the Empire. There must have been fifty thousand people here already, with more still pouring in above, below, and beside me.

But all of this I took in in moments, because my eyes were drawn to the scene of death and devastation below me.

Men and women fighting animals, dying in droves.

The Colosseum may have had more than five dozen entrances and exits for spectators, but the arena had only two: the Gate of Life, on the eastern side, connected to the Ludus Magnus, and the Gate of Death to the west, which led to the place where they stripped off the dead gladiators' armor and piled their bodies, and the grim cart eventually carried them away to a pauper's grave.

Still standing, looking out over the massacre, I felt my legs begin to shake. This was brutal, inhuman. How could my guys play a kid's game here? How could we play *baseball* in front of a crowd baying for human blood?

I felt Lucius place his hand on my elbow. I allowed him to guide us to our seats, trying to take my mind off the savagery before my eyes. When we reached our seats, I looked out to the arena floor just as a gladiator wearing a helmet with a visor but armed with nothing but a spear was attacked by a leopard. The animal rushed toward him and leaped toward his chest. The man had one chance with the spear and thrust it, but missed, and the leopard knocked him onto his back in the sand and was at his throat in a second.

I looked away, not wanting to see the end of that confrontation. There was a hand on my shoulder. I looked and it was Lucius. He smiled and shrugged. Business as usual. And my Wandering Warriors would be out there soon playing baseball. I didn't see how they—or I—could survive the day.

Under the arena floor was a maze of gladiatorial cells, wild animal pens, armories, and changing areas, along with shafts and pulleys and surprisingly sophisticated hydraulic mechanisms to raise scenery and wild animal cages and the like up into the arena. I'd spent several hours down there already, but the Wanderers would be seeing it for the first time today. I wondered what they were making of it.

And now they had to play some ball, my Wandering Warriors, in front of this huge crowd that, mostly, was lusting for blood. How would the crowd react? Had the Warriors built up enough goodwill over the past couple of weeks of exhibitions that some of the rowdy crowd would cheer for them? Or would my Wandering Warriors be designated as the bad guys and be reviled by the crowd?

I wondered how they were feeling right now, Quentin and the rest of my boys.

17

QUENTIN

Normally the Wandering Warriors would take the field by just running onto it. But this was ancient Rome, and this was the Colosseum, so of course it had to be very different here.

They'd marched us through the underground tunnel from the Ludus Magnus and lined us up along a corridor. I could tell we were under the arena by the pounding from above, and the dull roar of the crowd heard through several feet of sand, stone, and wood. The walls behind us dripped with moisture. It was like a weird cross between a dungeon and an underground bazaar, because people were running everywhere. Gladiators clanked by in full or partial armor, or naked with a net and trident. We could see and hear wild beasts snarling in their cages, lions and tigers and, for all I knew, bears, and we could smell them too. We could also smell blood and latrines and oil. And our own fear.

The Professor would have known what to say to calm us all down. Me, I had no clue. So I just stood there.

Fortunately, it didn't last long. One thing I'll say for Rome, it was a well-oiled machine when it came to running the Games. Everyone knew where to be and what to do, slaves and gladiators and lanistas and beastmasters, oh my Lord. So we only had five or ten minutes to stare at the floor, quivering and trying not to let fear overwhelm us, before someone gestured us onto a large platform which looked like it belonged in a factory, with gears and hydraulics and stuff I hadn't known the Romans even had.

The boys looked uncertain. I strode onto it without hesitating, just like the Professor would've. Then the rest of 'em followed.

The ceiling above us opened to reveal sky and admit a giant roar from a crowd that we still couldn't see. And up we went, the Wandering Warriors, to face our first game in the Flavian Amphitheater of Rome in front of a capacity crowd.

I damned near had a heart attack when the hydraulics lifted us up into place in the arena. Damned near. Because the place was *huge*, and the baying of the crowd was ugly. This wasn't a good-natured bunch of folks from the Midwest but an urban mob from one of the world's most degenerate cities of the age, bloodthirsty fans of gore and death. And now about to ... watch us play ball.

We'd need to make it good.

Right across the arena from us I saw another platform raising up into place. The Caelians, our opposition. I was gratified to see that they didn't look any less anxious than us. Upper-class Romans all, they'd never been in a full-up gladiatorial arena before, any more than we had.

"Okay, boys," I said, as our platform locked into place with a small rattle and shake. "Don't you mind that nasty crowd. We got us a job to do here. And we can do it. You all know we can."

I was pretty proud of myself, that my voice didn't wobble. I sounded confident. I didn't feel it. I tried to ignore the crowd, and instead looked around the oval arena.

"Bases already in place. Even a mound for the pitcher. Field's a little smaller than we're used to. But we knew that."

Suddenly I caught sight of patches of blood in the outfield, where men had died just moments before. I swallowed, cleared my throat. "So, looks like we're all set. Everyone okay?"

Everyone allowed that they were, though their eyes were big as saucers.

"Then let's get out there and warm up."

( )

As soon as we started playing, our Colosseum nerves all drained away. And, just like I'd said, it turned out we had no cause to worry, at least not yet. I went behind the plate, Walter came in from short to do the pitching, Duke moved from second to short, and our very own Co-Emperor, Geta, played second. The Caelian pitcher was a guy named Petronius Valens, who was an important Senator and used to having things his way, but his fastball wasn't much and his curveball was a joke, so we batted around in the first inning and then took it easy after that, trying to hold the score down out of pity. Geta had a couple of hits and did fine at second, and Walter just threw strikes and let the Caelians, a bunch of upper-class Roman men—and three women, two of them pretty darn good—hit the ball when they could get wood on it. Our defense cleaned that up nicely and Walter got himself a complete-game win, 10–0.

Walter tried hard to get them a couple of runs in the bottom of the ninth, getting one strike out and then walking three of them to load the bases. I made a big show of walking out to have a chat with him, and the infield all came in too. I gestured to Geta, trying to get across the notion that maybe we should let the Caelians walk in a run or two, let them get on the scoreboard. Geta shook his head no, pointed to the other team, mimed swinging a bat, shrugged, nodded. I understood, better to let them hit it, and play it straight. Which we did. Their batter got ahold of one and sent a sharp grounder to second. It looked like it had a chance to get through for a single, but darned if Geta didn't make a nice play on it, moving to his left to field it, then turning to peg it to Duke who'd come over to second for the double play. Duke gloved it while stepping on the bag and then smoked one over to first and that was that. A really nice double play to end the game.

That was the good news, but there had been bad news too. I was getting worried about Danny Felton on third, who was getting into it with the Caelians' third base-coach; a stout, old guy named Tatius who actually learned a few words of English just to poke fun at us. He'd been at some of our practices and now was yelling out, "Rag arm! Rag arm!" at Walter, who just looked at him and laughed a few times. But Danny, playing third, was getting annoyed, and he was the one guy on the Warriors, I thought, who might blow his stack.

In the bottom of the fourth, he did. A routine grounder came his way and he muffed it, the ball trickling away to his left. He took two steps to pick it up and then threw way wide over to first. That put the runner on second, the first time the Caelians had a guy in scoring position.

"Rag arm! Rag arm!" the Tatius fellow yelled at Danny, and that was just one taunt too many. Danny threw his glove down into the dirt and started walking toward Tatius with blood in his eye. Tatius squawked, he was no fighter, that was for sure; but the Roman bench cleared and they all came out to defend Tatius. I thought I better handle it myself, but by the time I ran down to third, clanking along in the tools of ignorance, both teams had converged and a fight was about to break out. The crowd was yelling in excitement; they thought it was great fun. But I was worried, thinking of that blood we'd seen in the outfield dirt.

I threw up my arms and yelled as loud as I could. "Back off! Back off!" and I think it was my size and that loud voice that gave everyone pause.

I walked up to Danny, who was still fuming, and I gave him the hook. "You're outa here," I yelled at him, all angry-like, and pointed toward the bench. Danny, bless his heart, settled down some, then said, "Okay, Quent," and walked away.

As he did, I wondered why we'd got off so easy. I thought

that was turning into a brawl for sure, and the Warriors always gave as good as they got in such things. Instead, one word from me and the Romans had gone all quiet.

Then I looked around and figured it out. Geta was standing right on the bag, elevating himself a little, and three of his Praetorians were right there with him, swords drawn. I caught his eye and nodded, and he smiled and nodded back, and we went on with the game. But Danny, I knew, was a marked man for the next game, the big finale.

But right at that moment, after that game-ending double play, Geta was happy like a kid at his birthday party as we all came in from the field and shook his hand and patted him on the back. I wondered about the protocol of that, since Geta's Praetorians were right there watching, but I noticed he waved them off when they started to pull those swords and, instead, took the pats and the handshakes and allowed himself to be happy.

We were happy too, but we knew we didn't have long to enjoy it. The Palatines and the Aventines were already being lifted up onto the field on those fancy hydraulic platforms, and we'd play their winner for the championship of the world, I guess. Nobody else anywhere in this time was playing baseball. Oh, and we were also maybe playing for our lives. At least we had an emperor on our side.

Anyway, we didn't need to watch. We'd seen all of them play plenty for the past couple of weeks as we'd played exhibitions all over the city of Rome and even beyond it, in Ostia.

Still, I wanted to make sure we didn't come up against any surprises, so I told Walter, who was probably done for the day after pitching that shutout against the Caelians, to stick around and watch the game and see if there was anything we had to worry about. And then they took the rest of us back down into the bowels of the Colosseum, and this time showed us into a room with benches where we could sit and take it easy for a while. Geta, of course, had disappeared off on his own, which was okay because although we liked him, he made the guys a little nervous.

It was a big room, and without Geta around we could relax there for a couple of hours, drink some water, even play a little pepper if we wanted, and then it would be time to get back out there and win the game that really mattered. Maybe we wouldn't have the Professor or Domna, but we'd seen all these Romans play and we didn't think there was any question about who'd win the game. That'd be us, the Wandering Warriors. I'd be pitching, and I'd pitch the game of my life. Which, come to think of it, it probably would be.

The question was: where was the Professor? And Domna? And could we get ourselves back home to our own time and place, after the game? I didn't have any answers to any of that. So I played some pepper with the guys.

18

THE PROFESSOR

I was relieved that the first thing I noticed was some cheering as the Warriors entered and trotted over to their bench. We'd made some friends, and I didn't hear anything too darkly negative from the crowd.

And then the second thing I noticed was that Geta was in a Warriors uniform! How the heck had that happened? And then as he took off his cap and walked around the infield waving to the crowd, everyone realized who he was and there was a huge clamor of approval and loud chants of "Ave Geta! Ave Geta! Ave, Geta!"

I peered more closely at the Emperor's box and noticed that Caracalla was pointedly ignoring what was happening on the field. He was busy chatting to the people around him, turning away to fill his cup with wine, glancing up to wave at the senators and other dignitaries behind him. Only when the tumult over Geta's appearance subsided did he turn back and make himself more comfortable on his wooden throne.

On the next throne over sat his mother, the same mother he'd punched the daylights out of last night right in front of my eyes. Domna was applauding as her other son walked around the infield waving at the crowd. Caracalla paid that no mind. But once she stopped clapping, he turned to her and said something, and Domna smiled and laughed and said something back, just as if nothing bad had ever happened between them. I'd have given a boatload of money to hear that conversation.

And then the game started, and it was the romp I'd figured it would be. Walter was pitching, and just trying to throw strikes. The guys played solid defense and hit the ball hard off that poor Caelians pitcher. But he stuck it out, to his credit, and went five innings before they brought in a reliever, the score already six to nothing and bound to get worse. The final was ten to nothing and could have been twenty-zip, but the Warriors took it easy on them.

The game was calm except for a little fourth-inning dustup when Danny lost his temper at third and Geta had to calm everyone down. And then it ended on an interesting note when Geta made a very nice play at second to start a game-ending double play. The crowd had lost interest in the game except for those moments when Geta came to the plate or when the ball went his way. That grounder was not an easy hop, and Geta had to glove it, move his feet and turn right, and then peg it hard to Duke, the shortstop covering the bag. Duke turned it nicely and got it over to first in plenty of time and the game was over, but not for the crowd. There was a mighty cheer from all fifty thousand of the men and women in attendance, sounded like to me, which was good news for Geta and probably for Domna too, if she could avoid getting killed by Caracalla right there in the stands.

I looked down there and Caracalla was fuming. He sat there, stone-faced, as his brother preened before the plebs, and then, after the Warriors left the field, he rose, took Domna's hand to bring her to her feet, and tugged her away as they left the stands.

I wondered if Lucius was seeing all this and looked over at him. He was, and "We go," he said, in English and so we went.

19

QUENTIN

They fed and watered us, down in our big comfy dungeon, just like we were cattle or horses or something, but no one gave us any info on how the other game was going, so all we could do was guess and wait until Walter came down to bring us up to date.

Which team would we rather play? The Aventines were gladiators, skilled and deadly fighters but not really baseball players. They came from all over the empire; captured in battle, mostly, and then sent into slavery where their one option for any kind of better life was gladiator school. The ones in the arena above us now were the best of the best; they'd survived months or even years of combat. And now they were playing baseball. No surprise, they played it to the death. Even during the exhibition games that led up to today they'd been dangerous. They'd happily run right over you at second, and I'd seen two plays at the plate that left the other team's catchers lying bleeding in the dirt. There would have been a third one, in one of their games against us, but Enos, out in center, had purposefully thrown the ball up the line so the Professor, doing the catching, had to dart away from the plate to go grab it.

Enos was one tough son-of-a-gun himself. He didn't mind

making contact on the field or getting right up in your grill with his teammates; but he knew he held the Professor's life in his hands after catching that fly ball in center and he did the right thing.

Despite our name, the Wandering Warriors weren't much interested in dying over a baseball game. Most of us had seen action in the Pacific or England or both, so we'd seen plenty of death and violence; stuff we didn't really talk about, ever, as we drove around the Midwest playing a kid's game. We didn't want to see any more of that here.

Of course, what we wanted didn't matter.

I was thinking of that when I decided to check on the other game. I left our big room under the Colosseum and did a hand sign to the guards that I wanted to see the game. One of 'em might even have smiled at that as he nodded and led the way through the rabbit warren of tunnels and finally up some narrow concrete steps into the bright sunshine of the Colosseum floor. Walter was there, watching the game, and I joined him.

We were behind a wooden barricade within twenty feet of first base, so I had a good view of the Praetorian Palatines, who were in the field wearing snappy uniforms that reminded me of the women's professional league back home with those kilty things that looked like short skirts. I looked up at the simple scoreboard they had in right field and it said, IV for the Palatines and II for the Aventines. I looked at the guard and he held up four fingers. I nodded. Close game.

And then I saw who was pitching for the Palatines, going into his windup while we watched: Caracalla.

Well, I'll be, I thought. He'd seen Geta playing for us, and had realized he had to get himself into the game too. And you know what? Old Caracalla looked all right out there. His windup was all wrong but he was throwing strikes and there was no one on the Aventines who would dare to hit it too hard, so Caracalla was looking good. Two pitches later, one of 'em turned sideways to bunt and pushed the ball right toward Caracalla. He charged it, picked it up with the bare hand, and pegged it to first.

I thought I saw him smile for just a second after he did that. The first baseman threw him back the ball and he raised it high in the glove and waited for his subjects to roar out their approval. When the crowd's response was tepid, more a murmur than a roar, he held the glove up again, with the ball in it, and turned slowly around to make his point. This time the crowd responded with the adulation he was looking for.

Well, it didn't surprise me none that he was a showboat, and I grunted. I heard Walter beside me do the same, and I said, "Let's go, Walter," and we turned around to walk back down to the room where the Wanderers were waiting. When Caracalla's Palatines won then it would our emperor versus theirs in the final. Now wouldn't *that* be fun?

I sure wished we had the Professor with us to help me sort this through. And having Domna there would help too. She'd know what to do about a battle between her two sons. Wouldn't she?

20

THE PROFESSOR

As we walked alone into the narrow tunnel, I suddenly realized I didn't know for sure where Lucius's allegiance lay. He'd obviously been taking orders from Domna when she'd sent him out to round us up at the river, but Caracalla was home now, and maybe he was calling the shots. I was unarmed. What if old Lucius had secret orders to kill me or usher me out into the arena with those gladiators grunting and hacking in mortal combat? I could just imagine how my pathetic attempts to defend myself would bring laughter to the masses. I'd never even held a gladius or a trident, a net or a spear.

But I survived the walk without a dagger in my back. We rounded a corner and there was Julia Domna. She nodded to me, but spoke to Lucius: "Your Emperor has decided to take part in the baseball game. And I am to take your prisoner with me."

"Julia Domna," he said, looking at her strangely, "I have no commands from your son about this."

I felt a shiver up my back.

"Now you do," Domna said. She reached out to take me by the hand. "Also, the Emperor wishes us both to play for this man's team against the Emperor's own team."

Lucius's brow furrowed. "But what if the Palatines lose the game they play now?"

"That will not happen. Even gladiators are smarter than that, Lucius. Caracalla will play for the Palatines, and they will triumph as your emperor hits the ball with the bat to end the contest in glory."

"Just so," Lucius said politely, and stepped aside. That all made perfect sense to him. As to who would win the finale, co-emperor versus co-emperor with their mother having chosen a side? Well, Lucius needed to keep his options open. He even wished me good fortune in the contest to come, as I walked by him. Sure, we were pals now.

And that was how it happened. Caracalla decided he was the pitcher and hitting fourth. All he could throw was a batting-practice fastball but he could mostly get it over. It should have been fat city for the gladiators, who'd been hitting the ball a ton in their previous games. But suddenly they were whiffing right and left or just laying down bunts. He walked in a couple of runs but that was it.

At bat, he went four-for-four as three fly balls fell uncaught into the dirt of the outfield and one grounder right at the second baseman mysteriously found a hole and trickled into right. So: three doubles and a single on the day. The only thing missing was the need for a home run at the end of the 8–2 game, but when he threw the final patty-cake of the game over the plate and the gladiator—a guy for whom death was a constant threat —swung mightily and missed, Caracalla took the ball back from the catcher and paraded all the way around the arena holding it high. And the stands erupted with thunderous cheering. I suspect a lot of the fans had no idea how contrived the whole game had been. Then Caracalla threw the ball high up into the crowd, and some lucky Roman treasured that ball for the rest of his life, I'll guess, sitting in a place of honor in the shrine to his household gods in his hallway. I wondered if it would turn up in some archaeological dig in a couple of thousand years.

QUENTIN

Well, it wasn't fun getting ready for our final championship game against the Palatines without having the Professor with us, but I figured we had to do what we had to do.

I told the fellas this as we sat on the benches in our big holding room and started putting on our spikes. "Boys," I said, "the reason we here are a team is because of the Professor. You know and I know that he'd be with us if he could." I looked all around, trying to see every one of them guys, eyeball to eyeball. There wasn't a bad one among 'em. "We know the Professor loves the game, and we know he loves his Wandering Warriors."

I took a breath and kept on going. "Look, boys, the Professor was pretty darn good at this game before the war, and he might still be playing in the big leagues if there hadn't been all that trouble. And I know about half of us went through that same thing. Some of us, and that includes the Professor—and me as well—saw some stuff we don't talk about. Awful things that we seen one human being do to another. Stuff so terrible it don't bear mention of any particulars."

Most of the guys were nodding their heads, looking down at their feet now, thinking about it. "Well, these here Romans," I said, "they don't know that about us. They think we're playing a kid's game." I paused for a second. "And you know what, they're right. We're playing baseball 'cause it's a lot more fun than shooting at people and getting shot at back.

"We lost friends in that war, and if things didn't make much sense to us, we still knew it was our job and we did it. Then we came home and decided to play some ball and look ahead of us, not behind. Now we're here and just like that war it don't make much sense. So let's just look ahead and not behind, fellas. Go out there and don't worry about things we got no control over. All we can do is play our best, right?"

There was a little murmur of agreement, so "Right?" I asked again, louder, and they all murmured again.

Just then, Geta and a couple of his guards came into the room. He held up his hand, saying hello to his teammates, and then he put his palm out toward us and raised it so we knew it was time to stand. Then the Co-Emperor of the Roman Empire led the Wanderers back out and up into the arena. And there, to our great relief, were Domna and the Professor! They were standing in the sunshine waiting for us as we trooped onto the dirt and sand.

You never seen such a happy reunion! Lots of handshakes with the Professor and cautious nods of the head to Domna. And then a hug between Domna and Geta. The co-emperor and his mother seemed very happy to see each other.

We walked onto the field, holding our bats and gloves up high, and then we walked completely around the arena to a great din from the crowd. Then, while we waited for the Palatines to do the same, the Professor and Domna and Geta disappeared. I was about to get nervous about that when they returned in uniform. The Professor wore his usual beat-up road grays like the rest of us. But Domna and Geta both came back without those Roman skirts on. Instead, they both wore long pants with stockings and the pants rolled up mid-calf and tucked into the stockings. It was great to see; just a little thing but it meant a lot to us. They wanted to be part of the team, they wanted to look like us. Like the Wandering Warriors.

22

THE PROFESSOR

Well, it was certainly the most important baseball game I'd ever play in, and I knew it as I came back out onto the arena dirt and saw that huge crowd cheering in anticipation.

The Palatines had already taken their walk around, holding up their bats and gloves, with Caracalla leading the way. And then, while we played catch and a little pepper to get loose again, the Palatines took some infield.

To tell the truth, I'd been laughing inside every time I watched any of the Roman teams take infield over the past few weeks. There's an art to it that requires someone who knows how to use a fungo bat, and not a one of them could do it right. Really, it was kind of painful to watch as their coach used a regular bat that looked about thirty-six inch and thirty-ounce. Hard to do much with that.

This was baseball, and in front of a big crowd where most of them were seeing it played today for the first time. I wanted them to like it, to get the full flavor of the game, to feel the joy of baseball, just like we all did. I was standing there, leaning on my fungo, shaking my head, when Quentin looked at me and smiled. "Maybe we oughta show 'em how it's done, Professor?"

I nodded. "Let's do that."

I walked over to the coach, a Praetorian that I hadn't met before. He hit a grounder, a clumsy one that went foul of third, out of reach of the third baseman, and then he turned to look at me.

"Can I show you how to use this special bat?" I asked him, and held up the fungo.

His eyes narrowed. I guess constant suspicion was the only way to a long life if you were a Praetorian caught up in the intrigue of the Roman court. But then he looked over to Caracalla, who was warming up nearby, and Caracalla gave him the nod.

So I caught the ball as he tossed it to me, and I gave those Palatines the sort of pre-game infield they deserved. They were out there, they were learning, they were playing, and so I gave them ground balls right at them, and grounders to their right and to their left, and then worked them through some double plays, including making their first baseman do it the hard way. Next, I gave them two quick final rounds, one of them some blistering balls that were meant to short-hop them, and then some easy pop-ups and some hard ones where they had to backpedal or turn and run for them. Then a finale of easy grounders they could field and throw to first and look good.

The Colosseum had gone quiet during this little display, but when those Palatines trotted off the field, they got an immense round of applause.

Then I did the same infield for the Warriors, and it was night and day. My guys were slick, including our second baseman and our shortstop, the emperors' mother who wore pants, and the whole fifteen minutes of infield was a joy to watch. I was proud of my Warriors, watching them work, and I even took the risk of a deep pop-up into shallow left that Domna had to get on her horse to catch, but she did it, over the shoulder, and the whole arena cheered.

And then it was time to play the game.

Umpiring had been a problem from the start. At the demonstration games, me and Quentin had volunteered to ump when we weren't playing, and that had worked out all right. At least we knew the rules and the strike zone.

When the Warriors were playing, what we'd done was get two Praetorians—one each from Caracalla and Geta's guards—to ump. We explained the rules to them and vowed that we'd help them fairly if they needed it, and we had them switch off each inning on who was umping the bases and who was calling balls and strikes. It worked out all right, though they stumbled a lot on calls at first. But they got more confident as the games went on, and by the big game I felt like they'd get the job done.

The question was, would we? Or better, what was the job that we were supposed to do? There was no question that we could hit Caracalla's pitching, his fastball was in the seventies and flat: batting practice stuff. And his curveball barely existed. We could, I'm sure, score all day long on him.

And on the other side of the coin, not more than two or three of the Palatines could actually get wood on the ball if Quentin pitched like he normally would. They were all right on straight-ahead fastballs, but Quentin threw a lot of junk, sinkers and curveballs and screwgies and changes and even a nice knuckler. They really couldn't hit any of those. No shame on them for that: they were hard workers, but they hadn't been playing it all their lives like my guys had.

So the question was, should Quentin pitch like that? What would happen if we won, say, fifteen to nothing?

I decided to talk it over with Domna and Geta, who were standing by themselves with a little coterie of guards around them, behind the bench. I walked their way and the guards crossed spears in front of me, but then together, mother and son, they barked a command and the spears opened wide.

"So here we are," I said, in Latin.

They both smiled. Geta asked, "Will we win?"

"We certainly will, Co-Emperor. It isn't as obvious to those up there watching, but these Palatines cannot match us in any respect. Also, we have the best double play combination in the league." And I grinned.

Neither one of them got the joke, though Geta was on second and Domna at short. I clarified, "We have you two on defense, and you both are very good." For beginners, I thought but didn't say. "And you both can hit their pitching." I looked at each of them in turn. "My question is, how would you like the game to go? We can control it. We can win easily. We can humiliate them. But we can keep it close if you like, let them score a few runs."

"We have seen battles like this in this arena many, many times, Professor," said Domna. "It is cruel, no matter how we handle it."

"But less cruel if my brother is allowed to play well," Geta pointed out. "If he hits a home run or strikes us out, mother and I, that would please him greatly, no matter the score."

Domna shook her head. I could hear her thinking. Geta, being nice again. Here, the empire was at stake, really. The two brothers had been away from Rome for years, and now they were back again, so first impressions really counted. Whichever one of them came out of this looking best would have an advantage with the plebs and nobles of Rome. If Geta got himself humiliated, it would be a disastrous and quite possibly fatal setback. For him, and maybe for us too.

Domna voiced her feelings. "You need to worry about yourself, Geta, not about your brother. Worry about your honor. Your future."

He looked at her. Geta and Caracalla had both been cruel when it was necessary. Probably, many had already died because of their decisions. And yet this young man, Geta, would make for a far better emperor than his brother. He held compassion and held Rome herself in as high a regard as cruel necessity.

"Veni, vidi, vici," said Geta, mimicking another great emperor. "But," he added with a smile, "let Caracalla have his personal successes even as his team loses the game. That will temper his anger."

In the history I knew, Caracalla wound up ruling Rome, and he wasn't much good at it. In fact, he was arguably the Emperor who started the long slide down to the collapse of the Western Roman Empire. If Geta could come out on top? I was pretty sure it would go differently.

And if it did go differently, what would that mean for us? When me and the boys got back to our time, would it be the same? Would there still be a United States that stretched from California to the Carolinas? Would there still be an armistice with Germany and would we still have used that superbomb to defeat the Japanese?

Would there still be baseball, or would there be some other sport to fill that bill as the National Pastime? Boxing, maybe? Basketball? They had a lot of fans, both those sports.

Or maybe there'd be gladiatorial arenas, with men fighting for their lives.

I had to shrug it off. I didn't know. Nobody did. All that was far beyond us. We just had to do what we thought was right, in the here and now. Live to the best of our abilities. Make good choices. Be our best. It's all anyone can ever do.

"All right then, I'll tell the boys," I said. "We'll control it and win it, but we'll make sure we give Caracalla some moments to shine. Agreed?" And they both gave me a slight smile and nodded.

I bowed to each of them and backed away to go tell the Wandering Warriors how we were going to play it. I didn't think I'd hear too many gripes. We all wanted to get through this last game and then get on home.

23

QUENTIN

It's been my experience that when things don't turn out the way you'd like, the best thing is take what you got and move on down the road. And that's pretty much what happened to us that afternoon in the Colosseum for the big final championship game between us Wandering Warriors and Emperor Caracalla's Palatines.

It started off just great. The Professor had talked to us all about how for our own sakes we needed to not make these Romans look too bad. And then he and I walked away for a minute to talk in private about it and he said, "Quentin, I know you'd like to mow these guys down, especially in front of this big crowd."

"That's the truth, Professor," I said. "You know there's not a one of them I'm worried about at the plate. I could dazzle 'em with all my junk and they'd just look silly up there."

He cocked an eye at me. "But you know we can't do that?"

"Of course," I said. "And I won't mind that, with most of 'em. But that Caracalla, I don't like him, and I got to admit it'd be fun to throw him a few curves."

"I bet," said the Professor. "And the crowd would love you

for it, Quentin. Hell, you're already the most popular player out there. They love you here."

"Yeah, they do," I had to admit.

"But Caracalla is the most dangerous one of the three. He's murderous, Quentin. He'd just as soon kill us as look at us. Hell, he's ready, right now, to kill his own brother and his mother. He'll do it in a second, if he thinks he can get away with it. So it won't be easy, but we got to get the boys out of here in one piece despite Caracalla wanting us all dead. And that means we have to tone it down. I'm sorry."

"I know that, Professor," I said, and then it was game time, so I turned away from him and walked out to the mound with the ball in my hand while he went to the bench to put on his gear. A couple minutes later I was throwing a final few warm-ups to him, and he was pegging one down to second, and we got things underway.

We'd won the coin toss and so the Warriors were the "home team"—ha!—and that's why I was on the hill to get things a-rolling. And that was fine with me. I figured I could dazzle them the first time through the lineup, and then I'd ease up for the second time around.

So the first three batters came up to the plate, and I sat them right back down with strikeouts. Nothing but curveballs, which they didn't know what to do with, so the first two went down swinging. The third, a smaller man I knew pretty well from watching him in practice and other games, liked to bunt and he did manage to foul two of them before I threw him inside with a hard curve and he backed away and then it broke over the plate. The Professor helped convince the ump it was a strike by catching and rising to toss the ball back out to the mound while trotting toward home before the call was even made.

Our guys took it easy in the bottom of the inning, the first two slapping out groundball singles and the third one, Enos, rapping out a double in the gap in right to bring them. Then we went down easy with groundballs to second and to third and a long fly to left that left Enos stranded at third but gave us a nice little 2–0 lead.

In the top of the second I had to deal with Caracalla first thing, since he was hitting cleanup. I gave him straight balls—I wouldn't call them fast—and he hit a sharp grounder to second that his brother fielded cleanly and threw him out at first. Everybody was happy with that. Then I struck out the next two.

And that's how it went for the next five innings, us putting up another couple of runs when Enos rattled a triple off the wooden wall in right field to drive in two, and me letting some of them hit the ball and throwing batting-practice pitches to Caracalla, who turned one of them into a double in the gap and the other into a lazy fly that dropped in for a single in left. The crowd was loving it—two Emperors and an Empress on the field, and some pretty snazzy ball skills that even a rookie audience could appreciate, so the plebs were going bananas and that Colosseum was *loud*.

Maybe we should have known it was going a bit *too* well. Yeah. Frankly, we should.

It was 4–0 in the top of the seventh when things got *really* interesting.

24

THE PROFESSOR

I thought everything had gone about as good as it could go. Caracalla's team was down on the scoreboard, but the big man himself was doing fine. And Geta and Domna were playing solid defense and each of them had a single, so they'd been productive and seemed happy. We were ahead four-nothing: respectable, but not embarrassing for the Palatines. Just the way we'd planned it.

But then, in the top of the seventh, Caracalla blew the whole thing up.

It started out simple enough. Quentin got the first guy up to foul out to me, a little pop-up behind the plate that was easy to make. And then the next guy took a mighty swing on an 0–2 count curveball and missed the pitch by a *mille passum*, which is Latin for one thousand paces. Quentin walked the third hitter, just to give the guy a chance to get on base, and then Caracalla came to the plate.

Quentin had been playing patty-cake with him all afternoon, throwing medium fastballs right down the middle so the co-emperor could get his bat on the ball. He'd grounded out to his brother the first time up, but had whacked that ball hard. Then he'd had a good hit the next time up, a double in the gap. Then

Bobby in left had done a nice job of not getting to a routine fly, and that dropped for a single.

Now he was up with two out and a man on first, so it was a good time for Quentin to put another one right down the middle and let Caracalla move a runner around. Which he did, swinging away on that first pitch and, to his credit, stinging it, getting the meat of the bat on it and sending a sharp line drive deep to left center.

Everybody started moving, Bobby in left heading toward the ball but making sure he wouldn't get there in time to catch it, Enos in center doing the same, Domna heading out to serve as the cutoff when the runner rounded second and headed for third, and Geta heading toward second base to haul in what was likely to be a routine throw from Enos, holding Caracalla at first.

Pretty standard baseball, unless you're a co-emperor and used to having things your way. As the runner rounded second and Enos reached the ball on the first hop, Caracalla didn't hesitate at first, but rounded the bag going full tilt toward second. Enos caught the ball and came up throwing, knowing he had plenty of time to nail Caracalla at second and end the inning.

Geta was in the right spot at second when the ball came in on one good hop and he gloved it cleanly and started to put the glove down to tag Caracalla, who'd be sliding in. But instead of a nice exciting play at second it turned into chaos. Caracalla didn't bother to slide but instead came in on the right side of the bag, full tilt, shoulders down, and bowled Geta over so hard that he sailed backward a few feet and landed flat on his back. But the ball was still in the glove and Caracalla had been tagged as he hit his brother. So, even as Caracalla stood up, the umpire, who'd been calling balls and strikes from behind the pitcher and so was right there to make the call, called him out.

Calling out a psychopath, and one of the masters of the known world? That took a whole lot of nerve on the part of the ump, but he made the right call. Even as he did, though, Domna and Enos were running in to see if Geta was OK. He wasn't moving and he'd hit his head pretty hard when he'd hit the ground.

You'd expect a brawl to erupt, and in fact a few of the Warriors had already started running toward second, expecting trouble from the Palatines and all set to defend their second baseman. But even as they ran, just playing ball, everyone else in the Colosseum realized what had just happened before their eyes. One co-emperor had purposefully attacked and hurt the other.

I expected the bloodthirsty Roman fans to be in full voice over this, but instead there was an eerie silence. It was so quiet that from behind the plate where I was standing, I could hear Domna talking to Geta as she leaned over her son to see if he was all right.

He was. Caracalla hadn't argued the call, since the ball was right there in his brother's glove, but he glared at the ump and then trotted to the bench, ignoring what he'd done to Geta, who slowly came to and sat up, eventually standing with the help of Domna and Enos.

As Geta got to his feet the crowd finally erupted into applause. Geta stood there, then held high the glove with the ball still in it and the crowd got the message even if they maybe still didn't fully understand the rules, and then the game went on.

25

QUENTIN

After all the hubbub at second base, things were surprisingly calm when we all got to the bench for the bottom of the seventh. I was sitting on the bench next to Enos.

Now, Enos was from Carolina and so he and I had a difference of opinion about skin color and baseball. But he'd fought on some of the same islands I had against the Japanese and we both respected that in the other. Enos had been an army captain and earned himself a bronze star by blowing the treads off a Japanese flamethrower tank in Okinawa and saved a lot of lives in doing it, so I wanted to like the guy, despite his attitude. And when it came to me and Walter—the team's two "Cubans"— Enos had come a long way over the course of the season. He saw us now as teammates, and I gave him credit for that.

But he had a hot head and he held a grudge, and for the last three innings Caracalla, who'd pitched in the first game and started at first in our game, had been behind the plate, catching for the Palatines. He wasn't too bad at it, but then he didn't have to deal with a lot of foul tips or even swinging strikes. When the Wandering Warriors swung the bat, we usually made contact.

I didn't like what I was hearing from Enos on the bench. "Ain't right," he was saying, and "dirty player," and "cheap shot."

And Danny Felton, of course, our team firebrand, was agreeing with him and playing it up.

Well, that was certainly true enough about that vicious play at second, but I leaned over to warn him, quiet-like: "Now, Enos, these guys, their emperor and ours, between them they're gonna run this whole Roman Empire. So we can't do one damn thing about that play except let those brothers decide it on their own. You know what I'm saying? Enos? You hearin' me?"

He nodded, looked at me, gave me a curious little smile and said, "Sure, Quentin. I hear ya," and then he went out to stand in the on-deck circle and swing a couple of bats.

I was hoping he wouldn't get into it with Caracalla behind the plate, and small favors, he didn't say anything to him. It'd be best, I thought, if Enos would just get himself another base hit and that would keep him happy and then we'd finish this game and get ourselves on home.

That almost worked out. Enos was up with Jake on second and one out and he went with the first pitch, ripping a sharp single into left. Jake scored easy on that but Enos had to pull up at first, where he stood there, a blank expression on his face.

He was taking a big lead at first, so the pitcher threw over there once to hold him, and that went OK. Then Bobby, at the plate, took a strike, then watched a couple of balls go wide, and then, as Enos went for the steal, Bobby smacked one hard into deep left center. And the Roman crowd, who were learning to like this strange game they were watching even if nobody ever drew blood, raised one hell of a cheer.

Enos was on his horse, like they say, and he never paused at second. The Palatines shortstop was out into shallow left center waiting for the relay from the centerfielder. It should have been a routine play, so he caught it, turned around slowly, and lo and behold, Enos was still motoring, not stopping at third like he should, but making a mad dash for home and—oh my Lord, I could see this coming—a collision with Caracalla.

The shortstop fired it toward home, where Enos was headed

with a full head of steam, and where Caracalla had come out to guard the plate. The ball got there first and Caracalla made a nice play catching it on a tough hop. And then here came Enos, not bothering to slide any more than Caracalla had at second.

Instead, Enos just put his shoulder down and rammed into the emperor, and sent him flying.

But Caracalla held onto the ball, and stood up slowly and, just like his brother, raised the ball up high for the crowd and the ump, to see. And the umpire—to his great relief, I bet—thumbed Enos out, and that was that.

Enos walked on over to our bench, looking smug, and I asked him if he felt better now, and grinned at him. He looked at me, smiled, and said, "Now that's baseball, ain't it, Quent?"

And I agreed that it was, but I was thinking, at the same time, that that wouldn't be the end of it. Caracalla was taking his applause from the crowd, but his face looked like thunder, and some of those spectators right above us were beginning to shout stuff that sounded pretty ugly.

26

THE PROFESSOR

So now we were at the beginning of the eighth and my guys were loose and happy—Quentin and Enos were sharing a joke on the bench, and Danny and Walter were grinning and punching each other's arms like schoolkids. Even Jake was smiling as he walked out to the plate, swinging his bat back and forth to warm his arm like he always did. Most of the crowd was happy too—the upper tiers, where the plebs were; they were Domna's crowd first and foremost, what with her sons being out of the country for so long, and Domna being on our team.

The senators and nobles, though, and the rest of the Palatines? That was a different story entirely. They were still seething about that play at the plate. Caracalla was obviously unhurt, and after all, he'd gotten the out and the applause for it. But I was sure it smacked of treason to the senators and the nobles.

I could see those worthy politicians bellowing and bawling up a storm, even as the lower classes raised a cheerful racket. I could see the fists waving and the red faces. And I could see them gesturing to the surly Palatines on the field, none too subtly.

Because those politicians knew how their bread was

buttered. They were either Caracalla's men already, or knew that their best hope of advancement—maybe even survival—in the coming months was to hitch their wagons to Caracalla as closely as possible, because he was highly likely to be the new power in Rome.

Caracalla was still pacing to and fro. I looked over to Geta and Domna. They were standing several feet apart, Geta with Duke and young Davey, and Domna out by herself, and they were both looking all over the place, eyes moving here and there, picking up all the cues from the crowd and the players that my boys were missing. Something was going on.

And then Domna starting shouting too, gesturing and waving orders. But it was too late, because the very next moment any semblance of this being a baseball game ceased, and everything happened at once.

The Palatines sprinted to form a group around Caracalla, on some signal that I hadn't seen. From their clothing they were pulling daggers, small clubs, metal knuckledusters. They lined up alongside him as he advanced towards us. I had the feeling he wanted to do a lot more than just get even with Enos.

Then, from the wooden barricade behind first base, a dozen legionaries came crashing out with Lucius Aurelius at their head, swords drawn, and made straight for Domna. They would reach her first. No way I could get to her, and no way I'd be able to fight them all anyway.

And even while all that was happening, and worse than any of it: over on the eastern side of the arena, the Gate of Life crashed open, and gladiators poured through it in full fighting gear.

Above and all around us, that crowd of more than fifty thousand lost their minds. All on their feet, all howling, they became a mob. Fights were breaking out all over, those down in the nobles' tier just as vicious as those of the street toughs up in the nosebleed seats. Within moments the match had been lit and the tinderbox that was the Flavian Amphitheater, doubtless filled with the coarser elements of Roman society to begin with, had flared up into a full-blown riot.

I wanted to run to Domna, but that was madness; it was my boys who needed me, and it was to the bench that I ran, beckoning them to close up around me too.

Not that it would do us any good. We might be able to kick the Palatines' asses at baseball, but they were elite soldiers, trained killers; in any kind of a fair fight they'd destroy us and leave us bleeding and dead in the sand. And behind the Palatines were what must have been a hundred gladiators, with even more streaming out onto the sand behind those.

Over yonder, Lucius and his men rapidly encircled Domna and Geta to form a protective cordon, practically lifting them off their feet in their haste to carry them to safety. Well, good for them, because this was no place for an empress, and I was glad she was safe and that Lucius had picked the right team after all. But that meant our last protectors had left the field.

So it was all down to me.

Sure, the Empress Julia Domna and I, we'd hatched ourselves a fine old plan up there in the palace on the hill, after we'd gotten all bruised and beaten by Caracalla and his thugs. We'd talked big while Rome slept, and thought we were pretty cunning for a while. But that plan had no hope of success now, not with the Colosseum a riot zone from the arena to the top of the stands, and a mess of legionaries and gladiators coming at us.

Sometimes, things just don't pan out the way you planned 'em.

But if we had to die, at least we'd all die together.

I shouted over the hubbub, loud as I could, "Warriors! To me!"

27

QUENTIN

I was gathering up the boys as best I could. Half of them froze in terror, half of them ready to run in any direction and get themselves spitted on a Roman sword. The Professor was bellowing at the top of his voice. Couldn't hear him worth a damn but he was trying to get the guys to come to him, and they finally got it and started grouping up around him, even though God alone knew what good that would do.

But now the gladiators split up. Those vicious fighters weren't all Caracalla's goons after all. Yep, half of them had come to flank the Palatines and add to their numbers, but the rest were running between Caracalla's line and ours, and turning to show us their backs. They'd flocked in to protect us. To hold off the Emperor's men. Among them I saw members of the Aventines team and some other fellas we'd eaten chow with in the mess hall of the Ludus Magnus. Even without language, we'd tried to be companionable as possible, when they'd let us. We'd trained together. Kind of. And now that was paying off. They'd chosen a side, and it was ours.

The two lines crashed together, two ranks of gladiators just twenty feet away from us, all fighting in a big old brawl rather than dueling one on one like normal. It was a crush of steel and blades, and some among them were already going down, gutted. Blood spattered. Heads were literally rolling. If I'd had time, I might have thrown up.

The Professor grabbed up a sword where it had fallen. Danny Felton had seized a trident from one of the dead. Duke was holding a shield, but he was so clumsy with it that I doubted it'd do him much good if one of those muscular, oiled gladiators ran at him.

We kept moving, sideways across the arena, all in a bunch.

It looked like the Professor was trying to move us west, towards the Gate of Death, and *that* made no sense, because that was the exit farthest from us and it was guarded by a stoic rank of legionaries who were declining to join the fray in the main arena.

And *they* wouldn't be letting us pass. We were going to die out here.

All kinds of stuff rained down on us now. Rocks and stones. Half-eaten chicken legs. Seat cushions. Those good old Roman boys in the stands above us were having themselves quite the time, pelting us while they weren't pummeling one another. With gladiators fighting and dying around us and the crowd rioting in the stands I had to wonder just how many folks were going to die here today. Aside from us, I mean.

The Professor halted, looking carefully down at his feet. What in hell was he doing?

Then the ground fell away just in front of us in a big rectangle, and my heart leaped. Of course! We'd go down on one of those nifty platforms, back under the arena, and then we'd …

But no. That's not what happened at all. I leaned forward and looked down into that rectangular hole as the hydraulics clanked and rumbled away below me, and couldn't believe my eyes. I literally thought that perhaps I'd gone mad.

Or that the Professor had.

28

THE PROFESSOR

Two of Caracalla's gladiators broke through and made a run at us. They'd killed the men they were fighting, split that line of gladiators who were doing their utmost to protect us, and were now pounding toward us. One was a lumbering secutor-type covered in plate armor with a heavy helm, his sword bloody, his shield raised. The other, ridiculously naked, was a retarius, armed with net and trident. In the brief moment I had to register it, I saw that he was also ridiculously good looking, despite the scars on his arms and legs. We were being attacked simultaneously by a tank and a Greek god, and behind them came four of Caracalla's soldiers, charging at us with swords raised, and a couple of the Thracian-type gladiators for good measure.

My boys stepped forward, all in a mess but bold as hell. Three of them were carrying shields they'd scavenged somewhere along the line. Three more had swords, though all of them were holding them two-handed like they were bats. The rest of the guys, well, they still clutched their baseball bats in their hands. A fine weapon for the gladiatorial arena …

The Wandering Warriors had stepped up to protect *me*, I

realized. Me, and one another. Because whatever the hell this was, we were still a team, and we were all in it together.

I was never more proud of them than I was in that terrible moment, with death charging down on us.

I risked a glance behind me.

Up from the bowels of the arena came our dilapidated old Ford Transit bus, large as life. I hadn't seen it for weeks, and it looked odd to me now, out of place. Raised up out of the Hades below, to bring us life.

Well. Maybe.

29

QUENTIN

We clashed with the gladiators. I was swinging my bat like a club and trying to whack that armor-plated guy's helmet, and Enos was thumping him in the chest with his own bat, while Duke tried to protect us both with the shield. But that secutor, he was actually *laughing* at us, and then his sword sliced into Bobby's arm and Bobby set up a wail and fell to his knees, bleeding bad. Danny Felton, he had stepped up to that naked retarius and was swinging his trident like a bat. Having no shield, the retarius had to parry that with his own trident, which made it look like they were somehow sword fighting with big long fork-shaped spears.

Danny was good in a bar brawl and he certainly wasn't lacking for any courage, but he wasn't fast enough. The retarius swung him a good one and knocked Danny clean off his feet. I thought he might just kill Danny dead with that trident, stab three prongs right into his chest, but instead he backed up and whirled his weighted net around his head.

The very next second, the net flew through the air and spread out, snaring Enos and Johnny both. They'd been about to take on a legionary or two, but now they were flailing like fish under that heavy net. Which, of course, was the whole idea.

Then the secutor jumped back away from us, startled, and

from behind me there came a very familiar wet cracking-sparking din as the Ford Transit backfired. It cracked a second time, and this time the engine roared into life.

All the soldiers were backing away now, and Caracalla with them, big brutish Caracalla with a sword in his hand and a mean look on his face, but even he was wide-eyed. It wasn't the bus's noise that caused it this time—the furor was so loud in the Colosseum that they might not even have heard that backfire from where they stood—it was that the bus existed at all.

What does a Ford Transit look like to a man who's only seen carts and, I don't know, chariots? What goes through his mind on first glimpsing something so massive and blocky, twenty-six feet long and nine feet high, and shiny? How does he know if it's a threat to him?

The Professor was sitting in the driver's seat, of course. He'd jumped down onto the platform while it was still rising. Even now the hydraulics had a foot or so to go before they brought it level with the arena's sandy floor. But our next move was obvious, and we did it. We grabbed bleeding Bobby and stunned Danny, and between us we dragged Enos and Johnny and the net and all back toward the bus, and somehow we all swarmed aboard it.

And so there we were ... in the bus. In the arena. In the Colosseum. Unless we'd mounted a roof cannon on the Transit or something—which we obviously hadn't—or were relying on the Romans staying spellbound by the Wonder of Ford forever —which they obviously wouldn't—I had no idea what was going to happen next. "Professor?"

"Everyone sit down and grab something," he said tersely.

And he gunned it, and off we went.

( )

The bus did not exactly leap forward. It sprayed sand and skidded rightward.

"Want me to drive?" I said. Couldn't help myself.

The Professor gave me the very briefest of irritated looks and tried again, more gently. The bus moved forward, wallowed rather, like it was wading. I wondered when the last time was we'd checked the pressure in those tires.

Out of the windows I saw the soldiers and gladiators continuing to retreat away. I was glad the bus's size gave them pause. Also, that they apparently didn't realize all this clear glass between us would shatter with a quick swing of any of their weapons. They could've mobbed the bus, clambered in, killed us all dead. But they didn't realize it and so they just stood there.

The Professor laboriously coaxed the bus around, double-clutched it up into second gear and then third, but it was still like driving in molasses. We lumbered in slow motion, toward the Gate of the Dead. Even so, the legionaries—no fools they—buckled and broke; they practically scampered aside to avoid us. Beyond them I saw a low tunnel that ended abruptly at what looked very much like a wall. "Professor …"

"Quentin, sit *down!*"

As we broke free of the sand, the bus lurched forward. That tunnel was only a foot higher than the bus with barely a foot clearance on either side. We skidded into the chute and it suddenly went dark, and the whole left side of the bus screeched and scraped against stone before the Professor, swearing, turned on the headlights.

We were still gaining speed as we thundered on through the Gate of the Dead. And I started saying my prayers while I still had time.

3 0

THE PROFESSOR

I had to trust her. She'd had this bus carried all the way here from the Tiber on a huge cart. She'd had it installed on the elevator, just like she'd said. Sworn all her people to secrecy, telling them it was all part of a grand finale for after the big championship playoff, a spectacle they wouldn't forget. And so it was, I reckon.

So if Julia Domna had also told me rather blithely that once we were out of the arena, we should just keep going and stop for nothing at all, that's exactly what I had to do.

Even though I was driving toward a solid wall.

A few seconds before we'd have crashed up into it and crunched the bus like a pretzel, the wall swung away in front of us, men tugging on ropes that hung from one side to open it wide as I downshifted from second to first gear but kept us moving. I'd known it was a gate—the Gate of the Dead, where they hauled out the bodies of the gladiators after their fatal bouts —but those bleeding corpses were hauled down the narrow sloping corridor that had just peeled off to my left and right.

But I guess they had to get their big carts into the arena somehow, that contained all the sand and supplies and such. The

Gate led to the outside, sure. And outside we popped, like a cork from a bottle, courtesy of some very last-minute action by some flunky of Julia's. Bless her.

Bright sunshine burst into the bus again. All of a sudden, we were outside the Colosseum, on its western side. Above me and to the right loomed the statue of Nero a hundred feet high, now converted into a more generic sun god, naked and gilded and with sunshine spraying out of his head. Dead ahead of us was the great marbled Temple of Venus and Roma. And beyond that was the Roman Forum, which was always packed with people. No joy for us that way, I knew.

I hauled the steering wheel left in a sharp leaning turn and heard various of my boys thumping up against the windows behind me and shouting out.

I didn't look back. I'd *told* 'em to sit down.

Besides, I had to concentrate. Out in front of me, Roman citizens were flinging themselves left and right away from the bus. It was now the full heat of mid-afternoon, and anyone who was going to the Colosseum today was already inside, so the crowds right here were pretty light, but still I had to slow down. These were ordinary people, families, workers; no one here deserved to be mown down by a giant five-ton vehicle from a distant future they couldn't possibly have imagined.

We lumbered on. I looked at the gas tank. Quarter full. Hoped that would be enough.

I skidded precariously around an arch, barely avoided a set of steps—in a city that relies on carts there's always a ramp some-where, and I'd scoped all this out on foot—and we careered south down a broad boulevard. The Palatine Hill rose steeply to my right, crowned with palaces, in one of which I'd dined with an Empress. Somewhere off to my left would be the Domus Vectiliana, where the Emperor Commodus had died, what? Just twenty years ago? Yes ...

A donkey cart was lumbering to get out of our way, but the road wasn't *that* wide. I managed to miss the donkey but clipped the cart good. It spun in the air, splintering in flight and scattering grain and wine amphorae everywhere. Whoops.

Well, carts weren't legally allowed within city limits during daylight hours anyway. Right? Really, that was all that was saving us from right now being stranded in the traffic jam from hell.

I barely glimpsed the Temple to the Divine Claudius as we rumbled by it, but here came the tall wall of the Circus Maximus, ahead and to our right as the road widened out into a triangular plaza. Just as I remembered. I honked the horn, sent pedestrians leaping and fleeing, and took a half-left out of that plaza into a much narrower street.

We were heading toward the city wall now. But we'd never get there unless Julia Domna had managed to pull off a little more of her secular magic on our behalf.

The road we were on led straight onto the Appian Way at the wall, but here it was a thin thoroughfare with high curbs on either side of the bus. The cobblestones were hardly made for twentieth century vehicular traffic, and even at twenty miles an hour we were getting bumped around and thrown all over the place.

But that was the least of my worries. In ancient Rome, streets like this flowed with open sewage. Even now, we were splashing through some vile stuff I preferred not to think about. And because of that there were high stepping-stones across the street every so often, so the more high-falutin' Romans could keep their pretty sandaled feet out of the mire.

Those stepping-stones were over a foot tall. Roman wagons had a high enough wheelbase to clear them easily, but they were way higher than the clearance of the Ford Transit. Hitting the stones would rip the bottom out of the bus and bring our getaway to a very abrupt and messy halt. But I kept my foot on the gas. Had to.

Ahead of me I saw more legionaries. Who now scattered as the Transit bore down on them.

"Ramps!" I shouted it aloud in my relief.

Up we bumped, up a very solid wooden ramp Domna had had made for just this purpose, and bumpety-bump we went down a similar wooden ramp on the other side of the stepping-stones. And in just two hundred feet it happened again: another bunch of soldiers, another pair of ramps. And once more, beyond that.

The third time, the bus grounded on the cobbles as it came back down to street level. We were killing the shocks.

I could hear swearing behind me.

I wondered how long it would be before we blew a tire.

We didn't. And now the Porta Appia, the Appian Gate, hove into view dead ahead.

And it was closed against us.

I was so focused on the street and on not hitting any of the pedestrians who were still jumping out of my way, even in the filth, that I didn't immediately see.

Within the gate was a door, just an ordinary people-sized door to let pedestrians in and out. We weren't about to fit through that. The gatehouse was guarded by soldiers, a full complement of legionaries who stood flabbergasted at the weird vehicle approaching them, even as we stared back at them in frustration.

I slowed the Transit, looked in the rearview mirror. We'd outrun pursuit, but if I was any judge of Caracalla's character, it wouldn't be long in coming.

"What now, Professor?" Quentin, of course. Good old Quentin. I didn't have the heart to break it to him that, after all this, it looked like we were sunk.

I braked to a halt, leaped up, threw the door open, bellowed at the soldiers. "Open up at once! By order of the Empress Julia Domna!"

The soldiers did absolutely nothing but stare at me.

Julia might have fixed the roads for us, but she hadn't been able to fix the gate. Or maybe she hadn't known that Caracalla would invoke some new law she hadn't known about. Those big old gates had sure been thrown wide when we'd first entered the Eternal City, and also when I'd been hoofing around it doing my reconnaissance for all this, just a few short hours ago.

"Here comes trouble!" Duke called out. Sure enough, out of the chaos we'd left in our wake came a swanky looking wagon pulled by two cantering horses, both frothing at the mouth. On the cart, soldiers. More ran behind, trying their level best to keep up.

We couldn't fight them. I was fresh out of fight. And if we abandoned the bus we'd never outrun them on foot down the Appian Way, even if the soldier-boys guarding it let us pass. It would be like a Chaplin farce. Until they caught us and gutted us, and it became a tragedy.

I shook my head, suddenly very weary.

"Professor?"

"What?"

"It's your girlfriend," Quentin said.

I looked again. Sure enough, sitting in the cart between two soldiers was the Empress Julia Domna.

She leaped down before the cart even came to a halt, running forward to shout to the soldiers at the gate. Even still dressed in her ball-playing garb the legionaries knew her, and you'd better bet they jumped to it quick as a flash. But the Appian Gate itself was pretty cumbersome and creaked open slowly, so slowly.

Yet again, I peered back up that road into the City, and here came more soldiers, a steady sea of them jogging after us with swords drawn, throwing pedestrians out of their way or just slashing them down where they stood. Yeah, those'd be Caracalla's thugs, all right.

Julia gingerly stepped into the bus, as if unsure whether it would allow her to enter. She looked at the shiny chrome, the twenty-seven identical cloth seats, two on each side and the three across the back, the rubber mats on the floor, all those glass windows. My big wide steering wheel, and the dials and glowing lights and gearshift. Only then did she look up at me and hold my gaze. "This," she said. "This is the real magic."

"Hell," I said, "it's just a crappy old bus."

She tugged at the door experimentally, but then I grabbed the lever on the dash in front of me to close it myself. I looked at the mass of Caracalla's soldiers pouring down the street toward us, and so did she.

At last the gate was open, and Domna—Julia—grinned. "Well then, Magister. Drive the crappy bus." She looked ahead at the Appian Way, cemented cobbles, wide and cambered, with its ditches and retaining walls, and her mouth twitched again. "Straight down the middle."

I looked at her, into her eyes, and said in Latin. "You're quite sure about this, Julia? Really?"

Her face turned somber. "I have done all I can. They are now their own men and must make their own way."

She meant Caracalla and Geta, of course. I nodded.

"And I do not want to give my life for Rome," she added, a little ruefully.

I didn't want that either. "Fair enough," I said.

The Appian Gate had a slight lip to it, so I had to ease the Transit over it. Just outside the city walls, a dozen street urchins stopped the game they'd been playing and stared at us.

Sticks and balls. Bases marked with rocks. A runner on first and the pitcher in the stretch, looking over there. It wasn't small-ball, nothing like. Me and my guys, we'd brought true baseball to Rome.

I waved at the kids, and rather tentatively they waved back.

"Wait, Professor."

Quentin pulled down a window and tossed out two bats, two balls, three gloves. The kids gaped even wider, if that were possible. Looked at one another, then stepped forward to accept their treasure from the future.

Julia looked back at the approaching soldiers and tapped her foot. "Magister …"

"Yes sirree, ma'am," I said in English, and winked at her.

Then I gunned the engine and it gave out a nice little backfire and off we went, the Wandering Warriors and Julia Domna, bumping down the Appian Way toward freedom.

31

THE PROFESSOR

It was the bottom of the seventh in Cairo, Illinois, and the Warriors were clinging to a one-run lead over the Egyptians in the second game of a doubleheader. We were playing two seven-inning games because that's how it was done for doubleheaders.

That part of Southern Illinois is called Little Egypt because of the two great rivers that meet in Cairo, the Mississippi and the Ohio, and because it's so far south, and so damn hot, that they used to grow cotton here. Cairo is pronounced "kay-ro," because that's how they pronounce it, but there's a Thebes too, and a Karnak. And the university's sports teams are the Salukis. You get the idea.

And those Little Egyptians can play some baseball. They'd been chasing us all afternoon. We were getting our hits: Julia Domna had two good singles and drove in a run both times, and everyone else was contributing too, so you'd think seven runs in seven innings would give you a nice lead. But not today. I think they'd seen Quentin once too often over the years because they were sitting on that curveball of his and knocking it around. He didn't have his good fastball. He said he was fine, but the pop just wasn't there. And we didn't have a good reliever, so he was just letting them hit it and counting on his defense, which

carried us along okay for the first few innings and then we stumbled in the fifth and sixth. Julia muffed an easy grounder to let
in a run, and then an inning later Enos out in center dived for a
sinking liner that came his way and missed it, so the ball rolled
all the way to the fence and turned an out into a triple, scoring
three more runs for them. And now, in the seventh, Quentin
had just given up a two-run homer, hanging one of those curves
up waist high and that Egyptian crushed it.

So with no one on and no one out, I called time and walked
out to the mound to talk to Quentin, mostly trying to buy him
a little time to catch his breath in the damp heat of Cairo.

The infield all came in too, slapping Quentin on the butt
with their gloves and offering encouragement. Julia, whose
English was coming along good in the month since we'd been
back, said, "Go get 'em, Quentin," and added, "Let 'em hit it,
we'll make the plays."

Quentin looked at her and laughed. "Thanks, um, Julia," he
said. We were all still trying to adjust to an ex-Empress being
our shortstop and wanting to be called "Julia." But we were
getting there.

And so was she. There were a half dozen other women
players in our league. During the war, the league had opened up
to women players; but there just weren't many of them playing
the game. Watching Julia sweep things up at short, I figured that
would change. A lot of young girls would see that they could
play the game as good as anyone.

In fact, that had already started, since that day we all woke
up back on the bus on the banks of the Sangamon River, back in
our right time and place. No time had passed in the world as we
knew it, so we yelled for the ferry and a guy brought it over and
we crossed the river and drove a few miles of dirt road to where
we picked up Illinois Route 48, which we drove like hell on to
get Bobby to the hospital in Decatur, Illinois. There were a few
of us vets on the team who'd seen wounds that bad plenty of
times and we'd patched him up pretty good. The docs in

Decatur did the rest, and Bobby pulled through OK. We sent him home to Hannibal and we'd pick him up there on our way north if he was healing all right.

After we left the hospital, we tried to get back into the right frame of mind by having breakfast at Emily's Diner on the outskirts of town, where they always served our two "Cubans" with a smile. After that, we all walked around town a bit to stretch our legs, and by 10 AM, we were at Fans Field, taking some batting practice and getting ready for our noon game against the Dukes.

Truth be told, I'd been a mite worried about Julia. She'd been staring around in a daze all morning, trying to absorb the shock of the new, even while the rest of my team rejoiced at being back in the world they understood. I'd left 'em all window shopping on Main Street for a few minutes while I ducked into the Decatur Public Library and headed for their meager history stacks. There I learned—to my sorrow—that Caracalla had still prevailed over Geta, who'd been sent into exile in Caledonia. That wasn't the way I remembered it from school, so we'd changed a thing or two back there, given Geta a while longer to live. But the end result had been the same.

By my boys' accounts, Geta had been a good guy. Maybe we should have tried to bring him back with us too, but I suppose he wouldn't have come.

As for Julia, I needn't have worried about her. Once she got to the ballfield, she'd shaken off her funk and played a solid game, with a single and two double plays, starting one of them on a tough ground ball that she gloved despite a bad bounce; and making the put-out on the other one, stepping on second and jumping to avoid the sliding runner while she fired it to first. It was great to watch. At the end of the game, there were a dozen people wanting her autograph, three of them young girls. We played the Dukes the next day too, and word had spread: the place was packed and there was a line of thirty people—daughters, mostly, with their parents—looking to meet Julia and get her autograph.

At the next stop, in Carbondale, there were twenty or more of those girls for each of three games, and now, here in Cairo, Julia had at least fifty of them in line after the first game and I could see them all yelling and screaming her name as we played the second. That was great news for all concerned, I figured. What I didn't know was that the local paper, the *Cairo Evening Citizen*, had heard about her too, and there was a reporter at the game. And that wound up changing things.

We won the game. After Quentin caught his breath for a minute or two he got the next guy to swing a curveball down low for a strike out, and then walked the next guy in four pitches. I stood up and was going to walk out to him again but he waved me off, pointed at me with his glove to get back into my catcher's crouch and play some ball. Okay, I did that, and he threw three straight fastballs, all three of them low strikes and with good stuff on them. The hitter watched the first one, swung and missed on the second, and then hit a sharp ground ball into the hole, where Julia, seeing it all the way from the moment it left the bat, ran hard, backhanded the ball and flipped to second, where Duke caught it, sidestepped the sliding runner, and pegged it to first in plenty of time. Game over, and on a splendid double play.

The girls in the stands went crazy, which was great fun, and then they all came down for more autographs and maybe just to be near their hero. Julia Domna trotted in from the infield, heading toward the dugout and maybe hoping to avoid the whole thing by going straight to the clubhouse, but I wasn't about to let that happen.

"These girls are your fans," I told her in Latin. "They admire you. Stay out there and wave at them!"

She did that, and then the reporter from the *Evening Citizen* came up to me and said, "You're the manager, right? I'd like to interview your shortstop, if that's okay."

Well, I'd known this moment would come one day. Julia's English wasn't really good enough for an interview, but by acting as translator I could hopefully keep things under control.

I introduced Julia to Paige Bly, the reporter, in Latin, and she agreed to the interview. They'd had news of a sort in Rome in her day, the Acta Diurna posted on pillars and walls, bringing the citizens of Rome who read up to date. She understood the concept.

The first thing that Bly wanted to know was where Julia was from, and when she replied to me—tongue in cheek—that she hailed from the Palatine Hill in Rome, I translated that as "I'm from Italy, where many girls play baseball as children." Which was now true, in my time, though I wasn't sure it had been before we made our little journey back to ancient Rome.

And that's how it went for the rest of the interview, with Julia subtly tweaking me and me cleaning it up to sound reasonable to Bly. This would work in town after town, I figured, until we bumped up against some reporter who spoke Italian, or knew Latin. And we'd cross that stream when we came to it. Lord knows we were good at crossing streams, right?

It went on this way for the next few days: another doubleheader down in Paducah, then a day off for travel before we got to Hannibal, Missouri, where we visited with Bobby Gamin, who was recovering nicely. The town's name was a lot of fun to talk about with Julia: a place named after a great African leader who'd damn near defeated the Roman Empire. There were bigger and bigger crowds all the way, in Cedar Rapids and Davenport, and good stories in every paper, and then we finally got back to Rockford, only maybe a hundred miles from Chicago, and so suddenly we were talking to the *Chicago Tribune* and the *Democrat*, and the *Sun-Times*.

Through all this Julia was playing better and better all the time and the Warriors were on a tear, winning five in a row and losing one, then winning five more. The guys were hitting with confidence, Enos was becoming a star out in center, and Julia's

English was coming along too. I really didn't need to translate too much anymore, but now that I'd built up the story as far as I had, I was enjoying the craziness. But I knew all along it couldn't last. And after the end of a three-game stand against the Rockford Blue Sox, this is how it ended:

Julia Domna was now leading off, and slapping the ball around, single after single, at a good .375 pace. Her glove work was good and getting better all the time, and her arm strength was improving. She couldn't make the throw to first from deep in the hole at short, but pretty much nothing else got by her. The crowds were overflowing the bandbox ballparks we played in and the papers were having a field day. And then, as we all walked off the field in Rockford and Julia stopped to sign autographs for the girls and their mothers, a woman I recognized instantly came up to me.

It was Grace Comiskey, owner of the Chicago White Sox. I stuck out my hand to shake hers, saying "Hello, Mrs. Comiskey," but she'd have none of that. She gave me a hug and said, "How are you doing, Professor? Knees holding up? You looked pretty good out there today."

I'd had a double, and done my job behind the plate, so I was able to smile at that. When I'd left the White Sox a few years before, the parting hadn't been all that harmonious. I'd had some knee troubles, and even for the backup catcher that's a bad thing. But I'd thought I had a couple more seasons in those knees, even with the years I'd lost to the war. Mrs. Comiskey and her general manager disagreed, and I was released. It all worked out fine, of course, what with my starting up the Wandering Warriors and getting serious about my teaching career and all, but it'd still left a sour taste.

"The knees are fine, Mrs. Comiskey, thanks for asking," I said. "But I'm betting you're not here to talk with me. Am I right?"

She smiled. "Professor, I'm sorry about how it went at the

end. But it's never easy for anyone when their career winds down, you know."

Well, sure enough. "I know, I know," I said, and then I saw Julia Domna looking at us and I sighed and waved her over. Baseball in wartime had made for a lot of changes in the game, including everyone looking the other way at the black players who claimed to be Cuban. In the minors, black ballplayers were playing openly, and in a year or two, I knew, they'd be playing the big leagues. But credit Branch Rickey for that, not Grace Comiskey, at least not yet. But a talented woman shortstop? I was certain that Comiskey was here to talk business.

Julia came over, and I told her in Latin that I was introducing her to the owner of a much better baseball team, a team that would pay her good money to play and make her famous. She didn't say anything. She already knew what fame was like and the good and the bad that came with it.

Comiskey reached over to shake Julia's hand and then put her left hand over their clasped right hands and shook them once, hard. She looked into Julia's eyes. "You're a little older than I thought. But you play like you're twenty. Great range, strong arm. Courage at the bag."

Julia looked at me. I said, in Latin: "She says you look immensely old. But she likes your defense. She says you have great courage."

"You will need great courage, Magister," Julia replied, straight-faced but with a dark twinkle in her eye, "once we are away from this woman."

Grinning, I turned back to Comiskey. "Julia humbly thanks you. She's from across the pond. Good old Europe. We're still working on her English."

"You tell her, Professor, that I'd like to see her at our spring training camp in Sarasota next March first. We're going to give her a good tryout. And I think she'll make the team, and that would make her the first woman in the big leagues. She and I and you: we could all be proud of that. Please tell her that, Professor."

So I did, and Julia smiled. If this strange woman wanted her to play, well, she was certainly interested. She told me in Latin to say that last part to Comiskey direct.

Grace Comiskey nodded, gave that quick grin of hers I remembered so well. "All right, then. Professor, I'll get the paperwork to you within the week, and you'll help her get it straightened out, right? Oh, and I like that Slaughter kid too, so he'll get an invite as well. He's a mean son of a gun, and we need players like that."

"Right," I said. Enos would be pleased. He had ambitions.

About to turn away, Comiskey paused. "And, Professor? We're losing Billie Northworth at the end of the season. He's retiring. Might you be interested in that job? Third-base coach? Help out our catchers too? If you want it, it's yours."

Well, there it was. A way to return to the big leagues and good pay for not doing all that much. Coaching third is about the easiest job in baseball: stop the runners, or wave them on home.

"I'll think about it, Mrs. Comiskey," I said warmly, but I was just being polite. I already knew what I was going to do. I'd help Julia get established here, let her finish up with the Warriors over the next month. Then I'd teach my classes in those long-dead languages, Latin and Greek, and do my research at Washington U. in St. Louis. Julia could stay with me and polish up her English over the winter months before she took the train south to Sarasota. We'd get along just fine, I was sure, me and the widow.

Then, with the spring semester ended and Julia Domna playing for the White Sox—the first woman in the big leagues, something me and the guys could indeed be proud of—I'd tune up our old Ford Transit, get the timing right with that distributor cap. Me and the guys would get in a good week of practice, and work a couple of new players into the lineup. Then we'd pack it up and head down to Kankakee, and Decatur, and Carbondale, and Cairo, and Paducah, and back up to Hannibal and Cedar Rapids and Rockford. Playing ball, making a little money, winning some and losing some.

Staying on the road, like we always did in the summer. Me and the Wandering Warriors.

AUTHORS' NOTE

As with many so writing collaborations, "The Wandering Warriors" had its origins in a casual, almost joking conversation between friends. At the time, Alan Smale and Rick Wilber were participating at the annual invitation-only Rio Hondo Writers' Workshop, hosted by Walter Jon Williams in a high mountain valley near Taos, NM. The dozen pro writers stay busy at Rio Hondo, critiquing and discussing one another's stories during the exacting morning sessions. But with determination and efficient time management, there's still plenty of opportunity for mountain hikes in the afternoons, and for long conversations over dinner and into the night.

Alan and Rick had admired each other's stories during the workshop sessions. And so, during one of those afternoon hikes, they—frivolously at first—wondered if there might be a way to combine their passions: Rick's for baseball fantasy and science fiction, and Alan's for all things Ancient Roman. They'd both won the Sidewise Award for Best Alternate History—Short Form for their work in those areas, so the idea of combining them didn't seem as odd to them as you might expect. In fact, they quickly became fascinated by the challenge.

A little research revealed that the Romans had indeed played ball games, in one case using a ball not much larger than a baseball. This historical tidbit provided vital grist for their storytelling mill, and by the time they'd clambered about halfway up one of those mountains they'd already mapped out the bones of a possible plot and pointed each other toward some key historical figures in both the classical and ball-playing worlds. Maybe it was the thin air at 10,000 feet, but the idea seemed to work, and they left Rio Hondo vowing to continue the effort. Their book contracts required them to focus on other work for extended periods—Alan's *Clash of Eagles* trilogy, which features a Roman invasion of ancient North America, and Rick's *Alien Morning* trilogy—but they still managed to maintain a steady back-and-forth on the story they originally codenamed "Amor Autem Basis Pila," based on rather bad Latin punnery.

And so, in the fullness of time, "The Wandering Warriors" emerged in its final form, telling the story of a barnstorming 1940s baseball team whose members awaken one morning to find themselves in Ancient Rome at the end of the rule of Septimius Severus, one of the Empire's last great rulers before its long, slow decline. Severus's wife, the Empress Julia Domna, is well known in our timeline, as are her sons, who inherited a split empire from their father following his death, leading to an inevitable and bloody conflict. The Professor of the tale, a Latin scholar and veteran of some secret actions during the Second World War, is also a real historical figure. The story of how he led his ragtag team of baseball barnstormers into the brutal heart of Imperial Rome to help Julia Domna find a solution to her problems, however, has not been so carefully documented ... until now.

—Alan Smale and Rick Wilber, July 2020

A TRADE IN SERPENTS

ALAN SMALE

A TRADE IN SERPENTS

"I would only add, that this Exporting of Felons to the Colonies, may be consider'd as a Trade, *as well as in the Light of a* Favour. *Now all Commerce implies* Returns: *Justice requires them: there can be no Trade without them. And* Rattle-Snakes *seem the most* suitable Returns *for the* Human Serpents *sent by our Mother Country.* ..."

—Benjamin Franklin, writing as AMERICANUS in *The Pennsylvania Gazette*, May 9, 1751.

The rattlesnake flowed out of the shadowy alley behind St. Martin's Lane, rippling like a strong sea, a whisper of the alien in the slither of its body across the grime and litter of the London backstreet.

Upwards of six feet long, with regular brown and gold diamond markings—*eastern diamondback,* thought Finny, heart crawling into his throat. Indigenous to a sunbaked wilderness halfway around the globe. By rights the beast could not even survive here, let alone thrive.

Let alone rule the streets of London, bringing the mightiest city in the British Empire to a craven standstill.

The snake headed directly for Finny and his son, homing in on their aristocratic blood as surely as a sailor's lodestone swung to face North.

The clatter of its dry, malignant rattle turned Finny's blood to ice. "Get behind me," he said to Simon. "Run."

"Not bloody likely," Simon said stoutly, but his voice trembled nonetheless.

Finny's swordstick had a forked end. He raised it—knowing the snake would attack quicker than he could react—and screamed aloud as it slammed into his waist. Straight as an arrow, fangs spread wide, the rattlesnake struck him and tumbled to the cobblestones leaving Finny unwounded, thick amber venom smeared across his leathers, and Finny, driven only by panic and instinct, swung the fork of the stick down just behind the snake's head, pinning it.

In theory Finny should now draw the sword from the stick and dispatch the foe, neat as Saint George. In reality, the diamondback was a monster of solid muscle, and it took both Finny's hands and all his weight just to anchor it to the pavement. At leisure, Finny would reflect upon the dangers of accepting the glib claims of Cockney weaponsmen at face value.

Simon danced, kicking at the rattler's tail until he could get a clear shot. Finny stamped and missed, the snake thrashing all the while, then Simon lunged in and ground its malevolent triangular head beneath his heavy boot, shouting "Hah! Hah!"—not laughter, but a demented war cry to hide his fear.

The dead snake lay like rope. Simon continued to eviscerate it, stomping its powerful body, its reptile blood smudging those bright diamond markings. "Enough," said Finny. "Simon! If we delay, other snakes may come."

"Bastards!" shouted Simon. "Let them come! Let them!"

Finny shoved the carcass into the gutter with his boot, but Simon seized up the snake and carried it to the coffeehouse in his bare hands. He spat on it and whipped it tail-first into the walls to shatter its rattle, punishing it even beyond death with a victor's righteousness.

Finny did not chastise Simon further. His son was fourteen years old, in the full blaze of youth, and this had been his first battle. "Good job," said Finny belatedly, and, "Well done," but Simon's bloodlust unsettled him, and he was glad to reach the door of the coffeehouse with no further incident.

( )

Malbon's coffeehouse graced the corner of Bow Street and Russell Street, just past the darkened stalls of Covent Garden. Nearby were the cheaper haunts of the tradesmen, but Malbon's was a cut above, a popular haven for brokers and politicians, wits and men of letters.

In happier times, a roar of conversation would have greeted Finny and Simon when they opened the door. This afternoon Malbon's was empty. And instead of the familiar *dame du comptoir*, Tom Malbon himself sat behind the counter, gloomily paging through the *Daily Courant*.

This was Simon's inaugural visit to Malbon's, yet he strode in with confidence. "See what we will endure for a pot of your most excellent coffee!" he cried grandly, and tossed the bloody snake onto the long wooden-topped serving table. Finny winced.

"Finny-my-Lord," said Tom in amused greeting. "The pup yours?"

"My son, Simon. Please forgive his exuberance."

"Gladly, if it brings me custom."

Finny ordered two dishes of Turkish Fine a penny ha'penny apiece, and the proprietor placed the pot on the stove. As the aroma of the coffee blended into the comfortable smells of mahogany, fire-smoke, and old tobacco, Finny's tenseness began to abate.

Simon propped open the snake's mouth with a spoon, and he and Tom discussed the beast's hollow fangs, only one of which had been broken by Simon's boot. The rattle was smashed to pieces, but Simon did his uncanny imitation of the dry chatter it had made when whole. Tom laughed; Finny shuddered. To his quiet relief, once the coffee was served, the rattlesnake was removed to the fire.

"They say you can eat the meat," said Tom, "but I know of none with the stomach to put it to the test."

Simon laughed edgily. "I'd cram one down Franklin's throat, perhaps. And another, till the man was quite full."

Finny took a gulp of the too-hot coffee. "Simon, let us not ... let us behave as gentlemen."

Simon turned to him, bright with excitement. Finny held his breath, wondering if his son was set to betray him. But Simon merely winked and said, "I apologize, Father," and the conversation shifted to lighter matters.

But Tom Malbon was a sharp man and well knew of Finny's Parliamentary connections, and Finny wondered how much more it would take for Tom to add two and two, and once he guessed their secret, what he might do with that knowledge.

()

"... *these venomous Reptiles we call RATTLE-SNAKES; Felons-convict from the Beginning of the World ... some Thousands might be collected annually, and* transported *to Britain. There I would propose to have them carefully distributed in* St. James's Park, *in the Spring-Gardens and other Places of Pleasure about* London; *in the Gardens of all the Nobility and Gentry throughout the Nation....*"

—Benjamin Franklin, *ibid.*

"I have oft been called a man of potent dreams," said Franklin complacently, thumbs hooked into his waistcoat pockets. "And aye, many of my best dreams come true. But these are directed towards the advantage of mankind, and come about through my own industry, and the toil of those whom I manage, in my modest way, to influence."

Ben Franklin did not have the air of a sorcerer. Broad-shouldered and thickening, balding and tending towards jowls, Franklin looked just like what he was: a newspaper editor and junior provincial politician. Moreover, his britches, stockings, and crisply buckled shoes made a relic of him, British fashions having recently lurched in the direction of tough dark leathers and heavy fabrics worn like armor.

The man's only uncanny aspect was his ability to talk about himself without cease. Interrogating Franklin made Finny's head throb, and their current session was well into its fourth hour. The two soldiers in the corner of the drawing room sat brain-numbed and slack-mouthed.

Finny pressed on. "And none of your previous dreams, nor your writings or predictions, nor any other of your pronouncements have come to pass in any ... *unnatural* fashion?"

"Never!" said Franklin. "Not in my lifetime have I seen an event that natural science might not readily explain. However, since we're covering familiar ground, let me repeat that I wrote my rattlesnake polemic in a most unusual frame of mind. As I composed my tirade against your government's policy of transportation and of the tens of thousands of convicted murderers, rapists, and thieves forced upon our young land these past years, brigands who then continue their loathsome careers upon our shores—as I crafted my prose, I was moved to such a state of fury that I dared not even blot my writing, lest I smear the ink. A thunderstorm crashing in the skies overhead found its echo in my soul. I was in such torment that my heart must explode—yet it did not. Exploded onto the paper, rather.

"And, aye, I surely used the organ of the press to curse my Mother Country, and indeed I wished serpents upon it—as a grim satire, a carefully-chosen analogy to drive home my message. Only to learn several months later, to my horror and confusion, that my curse had become true.

"Since then I have, as you know, recanted, and in print, but to no avail."

Finny suppressed a shudder. The rattlesnakes had welled up from grates and gutters, from flowerbeds and basements, and while they were chiefly drawn to the nobility, the common folk were not spared. By midsummer the death toll from snakebite in London had outpaced any other cause.

The confusion had not been Franklin's alone. None in England could guess the cause of the scourge. Eventually, news of the infestation reached the Americas, and certain information percolated back in the reverse direction, and the chain of events at last became apparent. But by the time British troops came to call at Americanus's house in Sassafras Street in Philadelphia, Franklin had fled.

Winter brought a temporary respite, but when the spring thaw came, the rattlesnakes and their new young again assaulted the streets of London, spreading out across the Cotswolds and the Fens into other cities. Transportation to the Americas had been discontinued, but it made no difference. Once activated, the daggers of vengeance were apparently impossible to resheathe.

Franklin was still in full spate. Finny forced himself to concentrate. "... Satire, aye, yet I felt neither wit nor subtlety in its devising, urged on as I was by the sure and steady presence of the Americans wronged, the Americans dead."

Franklin raised his hand to his cheek in a way Finny thought rather affected. "I speak metaphorically. But perhaps even then I knew I had brought about something extraordinary. Perhaps I felt a foreshadowing of the power I had unleashed.

"I believed that Providence drove my pen. Now, of course, I'm not so sure. But—please understand—I have always been the King's loyal subject. I have always loved Britannia, and have never sought to bring her harm."

"Indeed?" said Finny, at last getting a word in edgewise, and investing it with a healthy dose of irony.

Franklin smiled. "Remember, I traveled here at my own expense and yielded myself up to your government of my own free will. I came to lend whatever assistance I may, sir, as you must surely realize."

Another surge of sick pain in Finny's forehead. He rose and placed his hands flat on the table that separated him from Franklin, looming over the American. "*Sir*, I do not. As a matter of fact, I believe the opposite to be true: you came to gloat, to see for yourself what your magnificent but mysterious powers had wrought. To satisfy your curiosity and confirm your measure of your own importance. Do you deny it?"

"Certainly," said Franklin smoothly. "You ascribe to me a motivation I cannot even comprehend."

Finny narrowed his eyes. "Let us be candid, Mr. Franklin. You could never have escaped us. British troops stormed your house scant days after you decamped. We arrested your wife and your children, and interrogated them *most* thoroughly. We detained and questioned your neighbors. Thus, we quickly caught up to you. When you sailed from New York, our agents lined the docks and our men were installed in the cabins alongside you. Onboard, you had no conversations we did not overhear."

As Finny spoke, Franklin's face had changed utterly. His expression became harder, and the veneer of sophistication fell from it. *His family*, Finny thought. *That was the key.*

He drove on. "Had you attempted to hide we would have unearthed you and dragged you—and your family—to England in shackles. We would already have broken you on the rack. You would have kept back nothing.

"But do not think yourself secure. Even now, few men know your whereabouts: myself, the Prime Minister and his closest cohorts, a few trusted functionaries. We may still pursue a more dramatic method of extracting the truth from you. And if there is no truth to be had, well then, you have already been burned in effigy in every square in London. A few words in the right ears … The English can be merciless in war, Mr. Franklin. And do not doubt that we are at war with you now."

The new Franklin bounded upright and lunged forward to challenge Finny, eye to eye. The soldiers, awake now, stood also and grabbed at their sword hilts.

Franklin snapped, "A cowardly bullet in the night would be more the British style! 'Cleaning house,' I believe you call it? But perhaps you should beware, you and your precious Prime Minister and valiant countrymen! If I own the demonic powers you ascribe to me, I'm a dangerous man, not to be crossed, eh? Not to be crossed! Perhaps I shall burn *you*! Or summon snakes out from the walls right this moment, to do my bidding! Eh? Eh?"

"I doubt it," said Finny contemptuously, though not without a prickle of fear between his shoulder blades. "You have no idea how you did this. And maybe it's none of your doing after all. Perhaps a more powerful magician did it on your account." He eyed Franklin up and down. "Yes, I believe that's it. You're nothing but a distraction. A scapegoat. You're completely harmless, Mr. Franklin. Just another self-important colonial windbag."

The very air crackled. Finny did not so much as blink. For an instant he believed it had worked, that he had penetrated Franklin's defenses.

Then Franklin grinned, and the change rippled down through him. Civilization reasserted itself, his pugnacity draining away. "Ah, you goad me, sir. Did I employ an Indian medicine man to do my bidding? An old Salem witch? And would it solve your mystery, if I had?" Franklin shook his head and relaxed back down into his chair. "I enjoy your company immensely, Mr. Finny, but now you taunt me with trumped-up tales you cannot possibly believe. I fear we have reached the limits of what we can usefully discuss."

"I will decide that," said Finny coldly. "Who are you, Mr.

Franklin? What are you? Don't you want us all to know how clever you are? So tell me, man. Quickly, now."

Cool as milk, Franklin pulled out his pipe and studied the bowl. "You're floundering. Pass me along to your masters, sir. Let us take the next step in the dance."

Finny had been so close; on the verge, perhaps, of a breakthrough. But the opportunity had evaporated. Franklin was too much for him.

"Very well," said Finny curtly. "Onward and upward with you."

The brittle pause stretched to cover the best part of a minute. Then Franklin smiled again, and Finny reluctantly smiled in return, and the two men shook hands.

( )

"Send word to the Secretary of State," said Finny. "I shall await him at Malbon's."

The spy nodded, and left the room without a word. The guards were similarly taciturn. Finny wondered where the Pelhams found such solid mutes … and, if they could be persuaded to talk, what tales they might tell.

Enough. He was weary and his head was sore. Only coffee would ease the terrible ache that three and a half days with Franklin had installed there. Lost in his thoughts, Finny approached his private rooms.

—Suddenly, he heard the rattle of a snake, like Satan's tongue in a pile of leaves.

Finny spun and backed up, searching the thick carpets around him for the intruder. Then came the muffled wail of a child and a laugh that was almost his own. He strode to the parlour and flung open the door.

Alice, eight and tousle-headed, stood upon a chair with her hands over her mouth. Simon, six years older and approaching a languid elegance, lolled on the ottoman with a cruel and self-satisfied smile. At Finny's entrance his children turned to face him, Simon's expression transforming to butter-wouldn't-melt, Alice's to disappointment.

Because she always hoped against hope that it would be her mother returning?

Damn it.

"Alice? Explain."

"Nothing, Papa," said Alice, but her eyes still scoured the room's deeper corners. "We were just playing."

Finny knew better. Alice was deathly afraid of snakes, and Simon had just performed a perfect imitation of a rattler to terrify her.

He wanted to tell her that the code of the schoolyard was written by the bullies, that she should speak out if Simon were tormenting her. But he could not bear to see the derision in his son's eyes.

Frustrated, Finny pointed to each of them in turn. "Alice! Latin translation, Virgil's Aeneid, two pages. Simon! Fetch your boots and hat. You're coming with me."

"Papa?" Alice still stood on the chair, uncertain.

Ah, such a fine father he made. His son bullying his daughter, and his response was schoolwork for the victim, and for the aggressor … a cup of coffee.

Finny strode across the room and scooped his little girl up into his arms. Snakebite could easily be fatal to a child Alice's size. He felt her life in the balance every single day, and cursed his estranged wife for refusing to allow the children to go and stay with her in the country.

Alice was aquiver. He kissed her forehead and whispered: "You know you can't come, darling. It's too dangerous outside. You're safe here, and we'll be back soon. You're not frightened, are you?"

A forlorn hope. For Alice, snakes lurked under every table and behind every door. She awoke screaming so often that Finny had moved a cot for her into his own bedchamber.

"'Course not," Alice whispered back. "But, Papa, if I should become so …?"

Her words hung in the air. "Yes," said Finny reluctantly. "If you wish, you may go and see Mr. Benjamin."

It was all he could do.

"I don't even like coffee," Simon complained, as they pulled on their leathers and thick boots.

"Learn to," said Finny shortly. "The business of London is carried out in coffeehouses."

"I don't want—"

"You're coming," said Finny, with the absolute rule of fathers throughout the Empire, and the matter was settled.

( )

Now, it no longer seemed such a good idea.

"They say Franklin is impervious to snakebite," said Simon comfortably. "What do you think of that?"

"Folks can dream up a fine yarn about a man who's nowhere to be found," said Tom Malbon. "With no facts, rumors'll spread thicker than flies."

Simon took another swig of coffee. "D'ye know, I could learn to like this stuff. It really isn't so bad."

"It was supposed to be a punishment," said Finny, and Tom laughed, unoffended.

"So, come now, Tom," Simon persisted. "What would you say to Mr. Franklin, if he were here now, in front of us?"

"Wouldn't say nothing," said Tom. "I'd punch him in the mouth and tie him to a chair. Then I'd put a dozen of his favorite rattlesnakes into a cockpit, and toss him in along after, chair an' all, and see how clever a gentleman he thought himself then. And so we'd put your rumor to the test, young Simon, concerning his imperviousness. That's what I'd do."

"Would you indeed?" said Simon. "That does sound like a capital notion. Your thoughts, Father?"

"I say we are not Frenchmen," said Finny calmly, "and that no man should be punished without trial."

"I'd trust no magistrate," said his son. "For I'm quite certain that Mr. Franklin could twist his heart just as readily as—"

The coffeehouse door burst open, and in rushed five men with swords drawn, one clearly nobility, the other four surrounding and protecting him. They slammed the door, panting, and took stock of themselves and their clothing.

"Saved by the Duke," said Finny under his breath.

( )

"Nine of 'em!" cried Thomas Pelham-Holles, Duke of Newcastle, Secretary of State, and brother to Henry Pelham, the Prime Minister, as he stamped back and forth in front of the fire. "Nine!"

"Your blood must be richer than mine," said Finny, and stepped up to shake his hand.

"Ha bloody ha," said Newcastle. "I should be wearing plate armor and riding in an iron carriage. If any horse could be persuaded to trot through these snake-infested streets, that is." He threw his gauntlets angrily onto the tabletop and sat to allow his man to tug off his heavy boots. The other guards prowled the room, checking behind doors and under tables, scanning the walls expertly for spyholes.

"As a silver lining, at least London's rat population has been seriously curtailed."

But Newcastle was clearly in no mood to joke. "Come," he said curtly, and stalked off into Malbon's back room even before his crew gave him the all clear.

Finny caught his son's eye. "Don't get into any trouble," he warned. "We talked about this."

Simon just nodded and smiled and raised his cup.

( )

"Thus it may perhaps be objected to my Scheme, that the Rattle-Snake is a mischievous Creature, and that his changing his Nature with the Clime is a mere Supposition, not yet confirm'd by sufficient Facts. What then? Is not Example more prevalent than Precept? And may not the honest rough British Gentry, by a Familiarity with these Reptiles, learn to creep, *and to* insinuate, *and to* slaver, *and to* wriggle *into Place (and perhaps to* poison *such as stand in their Way) Qualities of no small Advantage to Courtiers!"*

—Benjamin Franklin, *ibid.*

"Pitt is breathing down our necks," said Newcastle once the door was closed. "His spies are out shaking the bushes. He guesses some game is afoot, but he doesn't know what. Should he learn we have acquired 'Americanus' and kept him close, Henry and I should be in devilish hot water. Please tell me you've made some progress with the man."

Finny grimaced as they sat. "I'm out of my depth, and that's the truth."

"As are we all in this sorry world. And especially so if a raggle-arsed American can blight us with the wrath of God. But I hope that's not the total of the wisdom you summoned me to hear?"

"Not quite." Finny steepled his fingers, marshaling his thoughts. "Since you dumped Franklin in my lap, I've spent long—interminable!—hours questioning him on all aspects of his background, his beliefs and opinions, and so forth.

"However you look at it, there's more to Franklin than meets the eye. Obviously, he edits and publishes his own newspaper. In addition, he claims to have also founded a library company, a volunteer fire department, an academy, a philosophical society, a military company, a hospital, and for all I know, a cluster of other miscellaneous institutions that have slipped his mind. He's served as Philadelphia's postmaster, and a justice of the peace.

And just before he fled the city he was elected to a seat in the Pennsylvania Assembly."

Newcastle eyed him shrewdly. "And you believe such a list?"

"Yes," said Finny. "Surely a little exaggeration here and there, some glossing over inconvenient details, but as far as I can tell the basics are true."

The Duke nodded. "They are indeed. That matches my intelligence. Go on."

"Very well. So, our Mr. Franklin gives all the appearance of being a solid, civic-minded citizen. A clever man. Pragmatic. Worldly.

"Despite that, I do also believe his guilt. Through his writings he somehow conjured up this plague upon us. But, here's the nub of the matter: I don't believe even Franklin knows *how* he did it."

Newcastle snapped his fingers. "I'm not interested in *beliefs*. Facts, man. Evidence."

Finny nodded. "Then let's consider the rattlesnakes themselves. They're clearly of unnatural origin; confoundedly aggressive, and active out of all season. The American rattlesnake avoids people and rarely strikes unprovoked, and could not survive in this climate. Our London snakes resemble them closely, but can strike quicker and higher than your American rattler. And the clincher, the unquestionable link to Franklin?— The snakes avoid him completely. I've seen it with my own eye."

"Go on."

During one of their earliest sessions, while the atmosphere between them was still cordial, Finny had invited Franklin to join him in a walk around his garden, believing that in a congenial setting his guest might let something slip. They had ambled among the rosebushes, with Franklin holding forth; today it was philosopher-Franklin, and he was prating at length on the Inherent Nobility of the Snake and its use as an emblem of wisdom, endless duration, vigilance, and true courage, and the resulting ironies of the infestation of London. Finny, half-listening, was making a mental note to have the rosebushes sprayed with vinegar to ward off bugs.

Then a rattlesnake barreled at them from the hydrangeas, propelling itself in an uncanny rolling spiral. "Guards!" called Finny, but the soldiers were too distant, and the snake was moving far too swiftly to be intercepted.

The snake rattled like hail on glass. Finny drew his sword, heart leaping. Franklin stood with his hands behind his back and regarded the creature with interest.

At a distance of a dozen feet, the snake halted and looked directly at Franklin. Its tongue flickered. It did not blink. Then it struck like lightning—not towards them, but off sideways, into the rosebushes and away through a hedge into the depths of the garden.

Belatedly, soldiers careered down the path. Finny waved them away.

"Sidewinder," said Franklin. "I've never laid eyes on one before. A remarkable method of locomotion, would you not agree?"

The blood thumped in Finny's ears, and he could smell his own sweat. Franklin regarded him coolly, his face displaying no hint of either contempt or sympathy.

For a mad moment Finny was tempted to run Franklin through and have done with him. But he sheathed his sword.

"Remarkable. And would you also agree that, in your own country and almost within your own lifetime, that little display would have proved sufficient to have you hanged as a servant of the Devil?"

Franklin set off walking again. "Then we must thank the Lord these are more serious times, and we are gentlemen not prone to superstitious hysteria."

—In the back room of the coffeehouse, Finny took a deep breath. "There it was. The only time I have ever known such a beast to approach and not complete its attack."

"Franklin admits his affinity with the creatures?"

"Franklin admits nothing," said Finny wryly. "For, in addition to providing us a perfect excuse for convicting him, it would be against natural science, and Mr. Franklin will insist until the cows come home that he is, above all, a man of reason. He has indeed achieved some fame as an inventor, having devised a novel type of stove, amongst other practical devices. Most recently he has indulged in some advanced speculations with electrical apparatus that have earned the attention of the Royal Society. His mind is unusually fertile, well ordered, and logical."

"You like the man," said Newcastle bluntly.

Finny sighed. "No. I find him completely impossible. But he owns qualities it is difficult not to respect."

( )

Alice Finny has a recurring nightmare in which she stands at the top of the staircase as rattlesnakes flow up the stairs towards her. Timber snakes and diamondbacks, spotted and mottled and banded in stunning hues of orange and silver, brown and green, they slither up from one step to the next, rattling as they come.

As the leading snake approaches the top stair, Alice clearly hears its scales gliding on the dark wood, and the dry, dangerous sound breaks the spell that holds her.

She turns to run, but behind her there is nothing—no landing, no doors, only complete blackness.

Alice teeters between the snakes and the inky dark. Then she tumbles backward, down the stairs towards the serpents, and wakes with a shriek and a start.

At this moment Alice Finny is well and truly awake, yet she has been so spooked by her brother's teasing that she still seems to hear the rattle and slither from her dreams. She climbs back onto the chair and looks all around, shielding her eyes from an imaginary sun. She pretends this is all make-believe, but her fear is real.

Surely there are rattlesnakes in their home, and Papa and Simon have left her to face them all alone.

Alice jumps down from the chair and runs to find Mr. Franklin.

( )

Tom Malbon brought in a fresh dish of coffee. The two men paused, waiting for him to depart.

Newcastle sipped and grimaced. "You drink this stuff often?"

"Constantly."

"That may explain a great deal." Newcastle pushed the cup away. "Anyway, while you've been *respecting* Mr. Franklin, we've sifted through a heap of intelligence gathered by our New England agents. They have found no shortage of reputable witnesses willing to assign demonic or, at best, unusual abilities to Franklin, even among those still ignorant of the creeping horrors he has unleashed upon London.

"Franklin was born just fourteen years after the Salem witch trials, and grew up not a day's walk away from there. That area is still rife with bizarre happenings. Yet, even by the standards of such a benighted place, Franklin's family—in particular his mother and some unsavory aunts—are viewed with unusual fear and suspicion. Disappearances, fortuitous accidents, uncannily bad luck, curses and blights … anything you can possibly imagine."

"Americans are prone to quaint superstitions," said Finny. "The colonies were founded in the first place by a collection of heretics odd enough and loud enough to be chased out of England." He paused, meaningfully. "Evidence?"

"The lack of evidence may be the strongest evidence there is," said Newcastle. "The Franklins' neighbors, both in their hometown and in Philadelphia, are so desperately afraid that they won't provide details. They're scared to open their mouths. That in itself speaks volumes."

ALAN SMALE

Finny shook his head. "I beg your pardon? You're losing me."

"They fear him, Finny, and surely not for his logical mind. Convenient enough to pose as a man of reason. What better cover, for a servant of Satan?"

Finny laughed. "You think Franklin purchased his many civic successes by making a pact with the Devil?"

"I didn't say that *I* believe it." Newcastle drummed his fingers on the table. "I'm reporting what *they* say, his neighbors and friends. Even his business partners accept the possibility. Unaided, surely no one man could be capable of all the achievements Franklin is credited with. And Finny, let us not forget why we are having this conversation. No normal man's words come true merely by being published. His intimate connection to this calamity is indisputable. Only the mechanism is in doubt. And there *is* no natural mechanism. For a God-fearing man, what other conclusion could there be?"

"What does the Prime Minister think?"

"Henry will believe whatever you and I tell him to believe," said Newcastle bluntly. "But, come now. You have been with Franklin for days. What else do you have? How would you assess the man's character?"

Finny quickly decided to be candid. With a prominent Peer of the Realm advancing the belief that Franklin was in league with the Devil, Finny's own private theory did not seem so outlandish after all.

Yet, it was still a ticklish idea to get across.

"His character?" said Finny. "You'll need to be more specific. For *I* believe that Franklin has several, all occupying the same head."

"What?" said Newcastle.

Finny drained his coffee and reached over to slide the Duke's abandoned cup closer. "Aye. Many completely different characters. Characters that make war against one another for control of him."

( )

Alice stays away from the walls, the corners, the curtains. Listening to her own racing heart, she yearns for the innocence of her childhood, when hiding beneath her bed was the shrewdest way to avoid monsters.

She sees no soldiers on her way to Franklin, but in her distress this does not strike her as unusual.

Alice enters Franklin's quarters.

Franklin is seated comfortably in an armchair reading a book, legs crossed at the ankles, eyeglasses perched upon his nose. He glowers at her in irritation at being disturbed. "How dare you?" he snaps....

Then the Change occurs, and the aloof, scary Franklin is supplanted in an instant by Mr. Benjamin, the jovial teller of tall tales.

Privately Alice views Franklin as a collection of boxes. If she waits patiently, the right box lid will always open.

( )

"When you interview Franklin, sir, observe how his demeanor can alter in an instant. An example: his two most diverse aspects are the politician and the scientist, and neither could ever be confused for the other. The politician is the most charming and persuasive gentleman you'll ever meet. He could arbitrate any dispute, lead any disparate group of men to agreement in a trice. Should he take a fancy to be King of America, I don't doubt he could rally a sizeable array of rich and poor to crown him."

"Charismatic, I'm sure, yet—

"Wait. Then broach with him the subject of, say, electrical phenomena, his current passion. In the blink of an eye, Franklin changes. He shrivels in stature; his attention focuses inward rather than out. He is immediately in thrall to an obsession, and here's the meat of it: he can no longer explain himself in straightforward words, but jabbers about electrical jars and prime conductors and negatives and positives and self-moving wheels and jostling water-drops in thunderclouds and Lord-knows-what-all. His other souls are literate, compulsive explainers, clear-worded men, yet *this* … The scientist in him cares naught for explanation. His relationship with electricity is intimate and personal, and if you cannot share it or follow his line of thought, Franklin scorns and berates you."

"I've known many men who—"

"Another example," said Finny doggedly. "I am a father. So is Franklin. He has two sons, and a daughter named Sarah of a similar age to my own Alice. The politician in Franklin may well kiss babies for electoral advantage and pretend to be solicitous of their welfare. The scientist might study them, with a clever treatise in mind. But neither man could even talk to a child, let alone raise one. I would not suffer them to share the same room as my family. Yet when my Alice enters the room, a new Franklin emerges who is a born father, who speaks to her on her own terms and instinctively understands her. *That* Franklin I would trust with her life.

"In a second, he transforms completely. Half a second! The Franklins are different in temper, in expression, in recollection, almost even in physical form. They are not mere moods or humors. I tell you, Newcastle, they are *different men*."

"I see," said Newcastle, sitting back.

Finny drank a mouthful of the Duke's coffee, for courage. "My conclusion is as follows: I believe there is a Franklin I have not yet met, and *that* is the Franklin who bears responsibility for our current plague of serpents. You must lure out and question that Franklin. Consult any of the others and you'll just waste your time."

"Finny, Finny," said Newcastle gently. "I don't doubt your sincerity, but this is utter balderdash. I fear the departure of your wife has unhinged you. Did you not tell me just a month since that she, too, was a completely different person these days?"

Finny gaped. "I … no, that was purely a figure of speech. I was … upset."

"By her desertion of you, and especially of your children." The Duke consulted his pocket watch. "I understand completely. By the way, I hear tell that she is suing you for independent maintenance."

Finny gripped the arms of his chair, suddenly adrift in dire seas, and Newcastle hurriedly added, "I mention it only so that you will be cognizant of how the women are gossiping. Eh? And I'm sure you're right about Franklin. But, *tempus fugit*. I must report back to my brother at Downing Street, before nightfall further increases the hazard of the journey.

"In the morning, I shall send my men to reclaim Mr. Franklin. Our committee is assembled: a couple of gentlemen each from the Cabinet and the Royal Society, a colonel or two, men of discretion all. And, in deference to your theories, I'll add a doctor and an asylum master. Rest assured that your efforts in this matter will be rewarded at the appropriate time."

The Duke stood, but paused a moment. "One thing I'll say for your notion. Franklin writes polemicals under a series of assumed names, each with their own distinct voice. Silence Dogood, Poor Richard Saunders, Martha Careful, Celia Short-face. Polly Baker. 'Americanus' himself." He shrugged. "It may mean something, or nothing at all."

"Celia Shortface?"

Finny found himself smiling. It seemed that, after all, at least one of the Ben Franklins had a sense of humor.

( )

"Thus Inconveniencies have been objected to that good and wise Act of Parliament, by virtue of which all the Newgates and Dungeons in Britain are emptied into the Colonies. It has been said that these Thieves and Villains introduc'd among us, spoil the Morals of Youth

in the Neighbourhoods that entertain them, and perpetrate many horrid Crimes ... "

—Benjamin Franklin, *ibid.*

Mr. Benjamin has just told Alice a funny story involving a talking goose. She never knew gooses had such deep voices. Papa never does this anymore, this relaxed happy storytelling, and Alice misses it.

She is still giggling when she hears a distant splintering crash from the front of the house, and moments later, a cry of pain.

Mr. Benjamin twists like an eel and another box opens; he is now a jerky, intense man Alice does not recognize. He springs up onto the balls of his feet and listens, alert as a terrier.

"Don't go," Alice urges him, afraid.

He waves at her to be quiet, and mutters his reply. "How could I? I am held prisoner here."

"But the soldiers are gone," says Alice without thinking, and then puts her hands up to her mouth at the awful realization. What if Franklin runs away and Papa blames her?

He shows no sign of doing so. She sees his mind racing and hears, from the hallway beyond the closed door, the sound of stealthy footfalls approaching.

"Damn it," murmurs Franklin, twitching.

She gasps. "What?"

"I think perhaps someone is cleaning house."

Alice shakes her head, baffled. Housework is much noisier than this uneasy quiet. She begins to walk towards the door—maybe the soldiers are returning—but Franklin hisses in frustration and shoves her back behind the leather armchair, where she will be unseen by anyone entering the room. Darting to the fireplace for a poker, he steps forward boldly and waits.

The door opens. Men glide into the room like winter shadows. Alice smells a sudden reek of mud and sweat and worse, and stops inhaling. A strong Cockney voice that might have been amusing under other circumstances says, "Hamericanus?"

"What of it?" says Franklin in a low grating voice and hurls himself at them. Alice hears a violent blow and a cry and runs around the chair.

Franklin crouches, clutching his stomach, coughing. He has knocked one of their attackers back on his arse, but five others surround him, vibrant with menace. They are ruffians, men of the docks and the alleyways, shabbily dressed, and they seem to fill the room to capacity.

Alice steps up and places her hand on Franklin's arm. She glares up at the rogues with unblinking imperiousness and says, "Leave him be, or my father shall see you hanged."

"Get away from me," gasps Franklin. Alice cannot tell whether he is addressing her or the intruders.

They push her aside and hustle Franklin towards the door. Then, "Bring 'er too," says their ringleader, a man slightly less filthy than the rest, with more of his teeth remaining.

"Cobbett, no!" one of the men protests, but Cobbett leans back and says, "Yes!" with a dangerous finality, the brass knuckles on his fingers glinting in the gaslight, and two of them reach back to grab Alice's hands, yanking her off her feet.

( )

The butler stands in the front hallway, flanked by two more of Cobbett's men. His eyes widen when he sees Alice and Franklin being frog-marched down the stairs. Another rogue stands at the broken front door watching the street.

"'Allo again, pal," says Cobbett, grabbing the butler's lapel. "Found 'em. Despite your sad lack of 'elp. My, but you're all clean and tidy. Shall I blood you, so you can tell of 'ow bravely you fought us?"

Not pausing for an answer, Cobbett draws his dagger and slices a long furrow through the man's starched shirt and into the meat of his chest. The butler's howl is abruptly choked off when one of Cobbett's henchmen whacks his blackjack across the man's neck. Alice, eyes closed, tries to keep breathing.

"Right then," Cobbett says. "'Ow's the outside?"

"All quiet," replies the lookout.

"Very good." Cobbett turns to Franklin. "Your rattlesnakes may be hell for business, but at least they keep the streets clear, eh?"

"You won't get away with this," says Franklin calmly.

Cobbett rubs his thumb and fingertips together. "Don't be bettin' on yer soldier-boys, now. They're long gone, spendin' what I gave 'em and pawnin' the house silver besides. I reckon they wasn't cut out for the military life anyway."

"We should have told Tom Malbon we have Franklin," said Simon, half-walking and half-skipping down the street. "Picture his expression!"

"You swore me your oath as a gentleman," said Finny sharply. "An oath that you came close to breaching."

"I promised I wouldn't tell a soul, and I haven't and shan't. Really, Father, even with a hint as broad as the Thames, Malbon could never have guessed it. For all the world knows, 'Americanus' is cowering in a bolt-hole in the Canadas. But just imagine—"

"Never mind!" said Finny. "No more imagining. We're washing our hands of Franklin, and thank God. Tomorrow he goes forward to a motley inquisition of soldiers, politicians, and natural philosophers, handpicked by the Pelhams."

Only a single rattlesnake accosted them on the journey home, a small creature like dark green ribbon that Finny nimbly dispatched with a stroke of his sword. But this splendid luck did not hold; they arrived back at Hanover Square to find the front door crookedly ajar, the butler prone and bleeding, and no trace of Franklin, Alice, soldiers, or maids.

( )

A broken-down terraced house off a dirty alleyway dappled with shadow. The rogues usher Alice and Franklin down slippery stone steps and through a door into a dank basement cluttered with cheap, decrepit furniture: a table, chairs, a copper bathtub, a packing case. The wooden piling that lines the walls is splintered and rotten; Alice can smell mold and other, more evil odors. The place stinks like dirty chamber pots and rotting rubbish combined.

Alice clutches Mr. Benjamin's hand. Despite the chill, his palm is damp. At first, he seemed unnaturally calm, and Alice took strength from him, but now Franklin shakes and breathes hard, and Changes compulsively.

Franklins come and go, advertised by the altering pressure of his hand. Each Franklin holds himself uniquely, contorts or straightens like a ramrod, clings to Alice or guides her, mutters or purses his lips.

Now, as they position him in the center of the basement, and the man they call Cobbett marches up to stand toe to toe with him, Franklin becomes very still. Alice cannot tell which box is open now, and this is perhaps the most frightening thing of all.

( )

"We need soldiers!"

They ran out into the street, as if help would magically appear for the asking. It did not.

Finny's mind was a void. He forced reason into it.

They had been betrayed after all. Villains had come for

Franklin. And, for whatever reason, they'd stolen Alice as well. As a bargaining chip? A plaything?

Finny only realized he had unsheathed his sword when he saw the blade wavering in front of his eyes.

Snakes were driven by blind instinct, but men could be cruel, sadistic, black-hearted.

Finny turned.

"I told nobody," said Simon quickly, backing up. "I hate Franklin, of course I do, any true Englishman must, but I'd never defy you, Father, never risk … this! Harm to us! To Alice!"

"Ridiculous," said Finny. "Stupid."

He seized Simon by the throat and rammed him up against the wall of the house. "Who else? You're a stranger now. Headstrong and vicious, always out for your own amusement. Who else but you?"

"The soldiers, perhaps …" Simon reached for Finny's hand and tried to ease its terrible grip on his neck. "Maid. Butler. Mr. Pitt could have learned … Any of dozens …"

"Did they give you money? Or did you do it just for hatred's sake? If Alice dies—"

"She shan't," said Simon. "We mustn't allow it."

And then, looking beyond Finny's shoulder, Simon's eyes widened. "The snakes, Father. Look at the snakes."

( )

Alice scans the basement for anything that might aid them in their plight, but sees nothing. The only way out is through the door they came in, and that way is blocked by five of Cobbett's dreadful men.

They peel her away from Franklin and sit her in a nearby chair, dirty hands pressing upon her shoulders to keep her still.

"You'll find us blunt fellows," says Cobbett to Franklin. "Plain questions, quick results. Get me?"

"I understand," says Franklin. "You're souls of the utmost simplicity."

Cobbett slaps him. "Don't need any of your lip. Nor yer filthy snakes neither. Tell us where they come from, and 'ow to stop 'em."

"Who's paying you? What will it cost to secure our release?"

Brass knuckles pound into his gut. Franklin bends double and spits on the floor, a ragged red.

"We're our own men." Cobbett grasps Franklin by the hair and pulls him upright again. "This is our city too. Our families are here. Our livings. Don't insult us."

Franklin smiles grimly through teeth flecked with blood. Little puffs of brightness seem to sparkle around him from the blows. "Very well. I understand. But, my good fellow, there's no single source for the serpents. No pipe you can block, no tunnel to brick up. They appear everywhere. Even your own people realize this."

Cobbett draws his dagger, still bloody-edged from the butler. "But you brought 'em. So you can tell us 'ow to be shot of 'em."

"Club them, cut them up. Burn them, one by one," says Franklin. "*En masse*, as a phenomenon? I can't tell you. I comprehend this little better than you do."

Without looking at her, Cobbett points the dagger out sideways towards where Alice sits. She cringes, even though she has been trying so hard to sit up straight and be brave. "All right, then. This 'ere girl. Mean something to you?"

Chills run up her spine.

"Tell us what we need to know, Mr. Hamericanus. Or ..."

"I'm not afraid!" says Alice, and her clear voice does not tremble.

"You'd harm a child?" says Franklin coldly.

Cobbett whips the dagger back and presses it to Franklin's throat. "I 'arm anyone I need to. The snakes, man. Talk to me."

◡

Only a few feet separate them, but when Franklin turns his head to stare at her long and hard, Alice immediately understands that he is saying goodbye.

Another Change is coming. This time the box opens slowly with an almost audible creak. Shadows move behind Franklin's eyes, sinuous shapes that Alice cannot fathom. For a moment he looks angry, and then sorrowful, and then his features begin to twist and warp until he no longer looks like a civilized man.

And perhaps even Cobbett is aware of the impending threat, for now he tucks away the dagger and punches Franklin coldly and methodically in the mouth, stomach and kidneys. With each callous blow, Alice screams and wriggles; fighting now, determined to help Franklin if she can or at least to cause as much trouble for these awful men as possible in the time they have left.

Cobbett steps away. He looms over Alice, dagger again in his hand, and stares into Franklin's eyes. "Well?"

On hands and knees in this reeking basement, coughing up blood, Americanus glares up at Cobbett and his accomplices and says, in a voice that freezes and crackles, simply, "*Stop.*"

"Oh, you're in trouble now," says Alice.

She is talking to Cobbett, for she can see that nothing of Papa's Franklin or her Mr. Benjamin remains. Power radiates from him. And he *outnumbers* them.

Perhaps Mr. Franklin is finally admitting a strand of himself that he has spent years burying deep beneath his other selves, for at that moment Alice hears him chanting words she cannot understand, in a voice she does not recognize; an ancient cunning, wrapped in an angry malevolence.

The new man within Franklin tilts up his head and raises his voice. He calls to New England, to the ancient ones of fire and water. He calls to his aunts.

The air ripples around them. Far above the cellar, the sky shifts. Franklin rears up on his haunches and lifts his hands to massage and weave the air, babbling.

The ruffians gape. Alice sits absolutely still, eyes wide. She knows that Franklin has already forgotten her name.

( )

The trickle of snakes became a flow. Rattlesnakes slithered down the street past them.

His red-smeared mind primed to kill, Finny released his son and walked into the path of a five-foot timber rattlesnake, ready to smash its skull. America squirmed at his feet.

Finny's blow never fell. The reptile slid fluidly around him, as did the next snake, and the one after. The rattlesnakes were no longer interested in spilling noble blood.

The men—for Simon must surely now be accounted a man, responsible for his own actions—looked at each other, and back at the snakes.

The wind rose. Storm clouds scudded across the sky. Dust and leaves skittered along the street. Wind, clouds, and snakes: all shared a single direction.

"Come along," said Finny.

( )

Alice hears a rattling sound and for a blessed, unreasonable second she believes Simon has come to rescue her. Until a rattlesnake, a brown-and-gold monster with a darting tongue, appears from a hole in the wall five steps away from her.

Suddenly the walls are alive, every movement a head shimmering, a body sliding. They pour into the cellar like deadly water.

Alice opens her mouth, but this time her muscles are too tight for the scream to escape.

Franklin leaps and whirls like an Irishman dancing. His fist cracks against Cobbett's jaw, and the dagger flies through the air. Then Franklin scoops Alice up and lifts her high off the floor with both hands, a floor that is quickly becoming a morass of rattlesnakes.

Franklin's eyes are wide. He is sweating and shouting something she cannot make out over the rumble of thunder and the hissing racket of the serpents. His rage is solid, tangible; any moment he may cast her down. Alice gulps and her eyes roll back in her head and, mercifully, she faints.

( )

Finny and Simon walked quietly amid the rattlesnakes. By now they were beyond terror. To Finny, they seemed to be almost floating down the street, with Alice somewhere ahead of them and only darkness at their backs. As yet, no snake had attacked them.

They turned a corner into a Soho alleyway, and now there was a real chance they might tread on a snake in the gloom. Finny found he was clutching his swordstick with a deathly grip and, in relaxing that grip, further realized he had left his gauntlets back at the house. His hands were unprotected, his sleeves gaped.

He heard a high scream and looked up to find three thugs rushing towards him.

The air was suddenly full of darting snakes. One after another they struck the ruffians, coiled springs that became lances, the hiss, the rattle, the stab. One man spun in the air, another tripped. Both went down, to be instantly submerged beneath a roiling sea of death. The third smashed headlong into the pavement like a falling tree.

A fourth thug high-stepped toward them, eyes wide, but more calm and careful about where he trod. Simon curled his shoulder down as if he were on a rugby field and tackled the man hard into the wall. Half a dozen snakes arrowed out to strike Simon from ankle to thigh, but he was oblivious. They fell away from his protective leathers and squirmed off into the night.

The ruffian gave a titanic twist that almost broke Simon's hold, but froze when he found Finny's blade at his neck.

"My sister," said Simon. "The little girl. And the American. Where are they?" He threw a hard punch at the ruffian's nose, in the process bashing the man's head against the brick wall behind him. He rapidly became cooperative.

"In the cellar, guv'nor," said the thug, pointing. "But the place is a nest o' vipers …"

Simon kicked the man's feet out from under him, dropping him to the street. As the snakes struck at the rogue's face and arms, chest and trunk, Simon snatched Finny's sword and slashed the man's throat open.

Without another word, Simon walked on.

Finny's ears rang with the boil and gurgle of the thug's death. He gaped at his son's retreating back.

Simon's valor held until he was at the brink of the stone steps, and then evaporated. Snakes flowed over his boots and down the steps like a waterfall. He reached a hand to the wall to steady himself and began to sob. "Alice! Alice!"

Finny did not hesitate. He went to Simon, gently reclaimed the sword from his shaking hand, and walked down the stairs to the hissing cellar.

( )

Only the force of a father's love could have propelled Finny down those steps.

The cellar stank of mold and rot, overlaying the bass reek of excrement. Finny stopped on the next-to-last stair and a cane-brake rattler lunged at him, fangs striking his jacket just above his bare wrist.

Finny hardly noticed.

Virgil, he thought distantly. *A Virgil translation, my last gift to her. How cruel and foolish.*

The cellar was ankle-deep in snakes, and still they came; out of the walls, down the stairs, through holes in the ceiling, up through the floor. It was a purgatory of rattle and hiss, lit only by a single swaying lantern that cast dull ripples of yellow across the unearthly scene.

Through his trance, Finny felt his eyes drawn to the one area nearby that did not undulate. It was a man's body, torn bloody, lying back over a chair. Clearly dead, the corpse continued to shudder as snakes struck at it again and again. Finny saw the glint of brass on the man's fingers, just before a snake's head flickered out of his sleeve.

Nauseated, Finny's knees weakened. He might have fallen or fled had he not caught sight of Benjamin Franklin, who stood at the far side of the cellar, grabbing up snakes with his bare hands and thrusting them into his pockets.

Finny blinked, rejecting the vision. Where was his daughter? What had become of Alice in this hell? He prepared to wade out into the churning sea of rattlesnakes, but could not bring himself to leave that final step.

The American's expression was as sheer as a chalk cliff. He wore no leathers, merely his usual dark breeches and stockings, and those flat-heeled shoes with high round tongues and large silver buckles. Madness.

Finny could see the shoes because Franklin stood in a clear circle, no snake within six inches of his feet. Again Franklin bent and plunged his hands into the seething mass.

"What are you doing?" Finny shouted. "Get out of there!"

Franklin straightened, a rattlesnake twisting in each hand, and glared at him. Finny shivered.

This was neither the politician nor the philosopher. Not the scientist or the father. This was a new Franklin, a Franklin of irrational power, spawned of witches. Finny did not doubt that he was at last seeing the sorcerer who had laid the killing curse of serpents upon England.

And his glare was pure frost.

I told him we arrested his children, Finny thought suddenly. He took a step back away from the icy shaman and tripped on the stair. Tumbling onto his arse, he felt a terrifying writhe-and-shiver beneath him as a rattlesnake squirmed free. Finny leapt up as the snake whipped wide-jawed into his knee and ricocheted off into the mass of its companions on the cellar floor.

Once again Franklin shoved snakes into his waistcoat and jacket. A rumble of thunder carved through the roar of the snake pit. "What are you doing?" Finny shouted again, his voice shrill with hysteria. "Where's Alice?"

For an instant the scientist in Franklin awoke and frowned impatiently. "I surely don't know." Then he dismissed Finny once more and returned to his absorption of the endless stream of rattlesnakes.

A third time, thought Finny. *If I ask a third time, maybe he'll tell me the truth.*

The cellar walls began to vibrate and flex, and Finny had the sudden image of the entire house transforming into a huge serpent, trapping them inside. The air thickened.

Franklin spread his arms wide. Finny felt a prickle along his own arms and shoulders.

"Franklin!"

—All at once rattlesnakes attacked the American, darting and stabbing him from all directions. Simultaneously, Finny was deafened by a giant roar. The stink of burning flooded his nose.

The building *jumped*, as if slammed by a colossal sledgehammer. Finny stumbled, raised his bare hands, and toppled forward into the sea of snakes.

( )

Hard floor beneath him. His son staring down, openmouthed.

"I'm all right," said Finny. If he was still alive, it must be true.

Simon helped him up. The cellar was blackened, the table charred, the floor ankle-deep in ash. In one corner the ceiling had collapsed in a mess of brick and splintered wood. The body over the chair was now a twisted charcoal heap, blasted beyond recognition. Of Franklin and his rattlesnakes there was no sign.

Hot pain drenched Finny's hands. His palms were burnt sooty. On his left wrist and the back of his right hand he wore the doubled red puncture wounds of snakebite, yet Finny felt no fever or deadening of sensation in his arms. He would live.

They found Alice under the upturned bathtub, wrapped in rags and dusted with fine ash, unconscious but unharmed. Unbitten. Breathing evenly. Simon dissolved into racking sobs. He snatched up his sister and fled out of the cellar.

Just like Franklin, Simon was a collection of miraculous strangers.

Finny walked slowly upstairs after them. Father and son sat on the curbside cradling Alice, looking everywhere but at each other. Simon snuffled and wiped his nose on his sleeve. Above them the night was radiant with stars.

"A lightning bolt," said Simon suddenly. "Like a snake, striking from the sky, straight into the building. Blew me backward into the street. Then a smell like nothing on Earth."

Finny nodded. "Franklin's doing. He was in there, with the snakes. He raised his hands and drew down the lightning, and that's all I remember."

A high-pitched laugh forced itself out from Simon's throat. "I suppose none of this should surprise us. After all, by Franklin's own admission, he *is* superlative at everything."

"Was," said Finny grimly. "No one could have survived that."

"*You* did," said Simon. "I'll wager that in a couple of months, our Mr. Franklin will pop up again in Philadelphia and resume his political career as if nothing untoward has occurred."

Finny recalled the snakes springing at Franklin from every side. "Impossible," he said. "Inconceivable."

Unless … the snakes had not been attacking Franklin, after all.

The weight of mystery became too great to bear. Finny stood, swaying as he lifted his sleeping daughter.

Simon said shyly, "I can carry her. If you like."

"No," said Finny.

On Long Acre they glimpsed a lone rattlesnake retreating into the dark, obeying its natural habit of timidity.

Alice stirred, her movements sending shards of pain through Finny's hands. He feared that she would awaken hysterical, but she looked around and took in the situation with calm aplomb. "He's gone, isn't he, Papa?"

Finny did not ask how she knew. He could no longer distinguish the remarkable from the commonplace. "Yes, Mr. Benjamin has gone, and taken the worst of the snakes with him. And the nightmares have gone too, Alice, gone forever. You'll always be safe now."

He paused, then continued firmly. "And, Alice, very soon, your mother will return."

Alice closed her eyes again, content.

Sometimes, saying the words can make them true.

Sometimes.

"I told Franklin a lie," said Finny presently. "I said we'd arrested his children. Treated them roughly. I invented it, just to provoke him. I surely wish I hadn't."

"I expect he realized that."

Finny glanced sideways. His son's stride was relaxed enough, but his shoulders were stiff and his gaze downcast.

"You *did* betray us, Simon. You did. Didn't you?"

Briefly, Simon closed his eyes.

"It's all right," said Finny, forcing the words out. "Under the circumstances."

"No," said Simon, desolately.

Finny sighed. "Carry your sister," he said, and guided his children home.

AUTHOR'S NOTE

Although my professional background is in science, I've always been fascinated by history. Not that this is particularly unusual; many of my colleagues in the astrophysics world are also history buffs, and at science fiction conventions I generally find that panels with historical themes are just as well attended as those on starships, robots, future war, and other more straightforward SFnal subjects.

So far, I'm probably best known for my alternate history trilogy, *Clash of Eagles*, in which the Roman Empire survives in its classical form until the thirteenth century and is now attempting to move into North America during the height of the Mississippian Culture. And, while some of my short fiction has been SF, fantasy, or horror, speculative history has been my true home for the past decade and a half. Most of my stories don't include known historical figures, but a few do, including the Brontë Sisters (and Brother), Florence Nightingale, the Wright Brothers (and Sister), Genghis Khan, and … Benjamin Franklin.

Unlike the lead story in this collection, "A Trade in Serpents" didn't result from a dare—no one challenged me to pen a tale that combined coffee and rattlesnakes. My inspiration came, as it often does, from travel—in this case a trip to Independence Hall in Philadelphia, which at the time included an exhibit featuring Benjamin Franklin's notorious "Join or Die" woodcut, that dismembered snake bearing the initials of the colony names, plus some information about an inflammatory and brutally satirical article the good Doctor wrote for the Pennsylvania Gazette, long before the War of Independence, and ... well, the rest is history.

I remember how quickly the pieces fell into place for this story—the magic, the psychology, and the family element: two fathers, adversaries from worlds far apart, who reach an odd understanding through their love for their children. The tale did morph in the telling, but Alice always remained the emotional center.

I'm grateful to Shawna McCarthy, fiction editor at *Realms of Fantasy*, for publishing this story and five others of mine between 1998 and 2011. *Realms* was a really neat magazine, and I still miss it.

—Alan Smale, June 2020

STEPHEN TO CORA TO JOE, OR, THE TRUTH AS I KNOW IT

RICK WILBER

1

STEPHEN TO CORA TO JOE, OR, THE TRUTH AS I KNOW IT

On a Sunday afternoon in September that threatened a downpour, in the top of the eighth of the last game of the season, with no one on and two outs and things pretty much looking okay, suddenly I couldn't find the strike zone.

Control tells you the truth about yourself. You go along thinking you know exactly where to place the ball and you're always getting it in there, and then suddenly you can't find the damn plate. Sliders that had painted the black just the inning before started missing wide or were down in the dirt, and my fastball—such as it is—lost the corners, coming in so fat I had to quit using it or risk someone coming back up the middle with a line drive and taking my head off.

I walked the first guy in the inning on four pitches, two of them way wide and two in the dirt. He was their number seven hitter and I'd gotten him out three other times on easy groundballs. Now I'd walked him on four straight. Steve, back behind the plate, was not happy about that.

As the batter trotted down to first, Steve came clanking out, the broken metal clasps of the cheap shin guards I'd bought him at the used sporting goods store rattling loosely. There was an ominous rumble of thunder from a squall line out over the bay. I looked that way, took a deep breath, tried to think my way through my control troubles by looking at the scenery. A rainbow was just forming, a thin arc of color emerging in front of the charcoal sheets of rain. Just a bit south of that, a huge mass of low blue-gray clouds boiled, the sky running from pewter to dangerous shades of green and black.

"Looks quite mean and low out there, David, don't it?" Steve said in that Bronx jargon he put on for laughs sometimes. "But, hully gee, I don't think she's blowing our way." He slipped his catcher's mask up on top of his head and then held the ball out to me, nestled in that wide Rawlings mitt I'd bought him. "So, ya mug," he added, "how ya feeling?"

I looked over toward the stands. Cora was there, watching us, wearing a Rays cap in our honor, and sitting up straight on the bleacher seat so I couldn't miss the tight scoop-neck T-shirt, those glossy sports shorts she likes, and her granny sunglasses set up on the top of that blond hair. She looked gorgeous. She saw me seeing her, gave me a quick wave of her hand, and smiled. Next to her on the grandstand bench was a small overnight bag. That, I thought, was a good indicator.

I turned to look at Steve. "I'm fine," I said. "Just lost it for a second there, that's all. It's been a long day."

Steve had seen where I was looking. "David, Cora's a real looker, got a real shape on her, she does." He grinned. "She's got everything an old fart like you could want, including that ample bosom, but if you don't start worrying about your pitching, I'll lam the head off ya. Got it? We're two runs in front and this is the bottom of their order. Just throw the old pellet in there and let them hit it, right? Let your fielders do their job."

I nodded. "Sure. Let them hit it." That plan, I thought, gave our defense more credit than it was due, but I didn't say that. It was always hard for me to argue with Steve.

He leaned in close, stared at me hard, eyes narrowing. "Don't be rum, David. We don't have anyone in relief. It's your game, win or lose, all right?"

"I'm fine, Steve. Really. Let's get this guy." I was tense, and he could sense it. He was good at that. He smiled. "Loosen up," he said, "and just throw strikes."

He turned to walk back, stopped, turned back. "Did I ever tell you what my friend Joseph said about America's love for base ball?"

I smiled back. "Joseph? Conrad? No, you never did." Steve loved telling those stories about his circle of friends when he lived in England: Henry James, Ford Madox Ford, H.G. Wells, Conrad—they were all his pals there at Brede Manor down in Sussex, south of London, in that last year of Steve's life as he slowly died from the consumption that destroyed his lungs. It must have been quite a group when they got together on a Saturday evening to drink, smoke, and play cards and listen to the rattle of Steve's cough.

I wanted to hear the story, but then the ump walked out and made us break it up and get back to the business at hand. I walked the next guy too, and then gave up a double and a single before finding my nerve and settling back down with us a run down. We tied it up on Steve's single in the ninth before the squall line hit and the rain came down and everything got very confused.

I never did get to hear what Conrad had to say about baseball.

2

HER UPTURNED FACE

I first met Cora on a Monday morning as I walked across campus from my office in the Arts Building to Taylor Hall, where I taught a 9 AM class in Fiction Writing 402, Advanced Techniques for the Short Story.

She sat on the low brick wall that marks the path between the two buildings, reading a thin, little book. She wore a tight T-shirt that showed off her breasts, a pair of plaid walking shorts, and those platform sandals that are so popular with the coeds these days. She had broad features; there's nothing delicate about Cora, with that wide mouth and her red lipstick. It was too much makeup, but she wore it well.

As I walked by, she looked up at me; that beautiful upturned face, her eyes wide, those lips pouty and full. "Professor Holman?"

I just smiled at first. I'd been teaching a long time, and you develop a kind of immunity to the sexual displays of the typical undergraduate. But then, I swear it, she said this: "The burnt sky thundered its rejection of Sean's entreaty. Nature, inimical Nature, arched her back and hissed at him. Her claws were out. He felt small, and still shrinking. Great cracks of fury pounded him, reducing him, until he was gone."

My jaw must have dropped. "Wow," I said. "You've actually read that?" It was from "Hide the Monster," the title story from my thin little collection, part of my Big Break five years before: a two-book deal, the short story collection with the novel to follow. The collection got some nice reviews in places that matter and sold well; the novel I'm almost done with and my agent and my editor love what they've seen of it.

"I love that story," she said, and held out the book she was reading. It was the collection. "I've memorized whole passages from these stories. Will you autograph the book for me?"

I laughed. "Does rain fall from the cracked sky? Hand that over, dear."

And I found out her name so I could sign: "To Cora Taylor, A Beautiful Reader." She giggled at that when she read it, then thanked me, said she thought the book was the best thing she'd read in years and that she'd been surprised to find I was teaching right here on campus. I thanked her again, and we kept talking. She flirted. I flirted back, and then met her for drinks a few hours later and we wound up in bed.

It was all very simple, very effortless. Have you ever noticed how all the best things seem to just fall into your lap and that the things you try for the hardest are the ones hardest to get? It's always been that way for me, and Cora was a perfect example. A girl like that? Wanting to bed a tired, old writer like me? It was laughable until it happened, and then it all seemed perfectly normal, like I knew what I was doing, like I had it all under control.

3
<hr>

ACTIVE SERVICE

There was a time when I could really play The Game. Pitcher for the national champs in college at Southern Illinois, four years in the minors after that in places like Paintsville, Kentucky, where I met Emily, the perfect girl for a young pitcher; and then in Lakeland, Florida, and Medford, Oregon, where I could show her off along with my skills.

And then came my cup of coffee in The Show when the Cardinals called me up in September with the expanded roster and I got my shot. It didn't take me long to figure out that I was good, not great, on a pitching staff that took the Cards to the World Series. My career stats: no wins, two losses, an ERA of 4.05.

I was on the big league roster for spring training the next season but couldn't stick. Then I went down to Triple A and couldn't find the plate. Same at Double A and while I kept at it for another year or two after that, the two truths I discovered were these: the downslope is a slick one and twenty-eight is an old man for a minor leaguer. So before I was thirty, I had to face doing something with the rest of my life. I thought I'd make a good college coach, and that meant getting some degrees, so I went back to school, got one degree and then another and then still another while I got interested in words and how they're put together, and I started caring about writing. Baseball—that other life—disappeared into my past until finally, on the day I sold my first short story to the *Mississippi Review*, I didn't pay attention to it anymore at all. It was fifteen years before I came back to it.

4

FAST RODE THE KNIGHT

Steve rowed up to practice the day I met him. We were two weeks away from our first game, and I was running in the outfield, trying to loosen up some old tendons and build up a little endurance at the same time. We play in an over-thirty league, all very amateur; doctors and lawyers and teachers and mechanics and salesmen and even one politician, a city councilman who has his eyes on the mayor's office. We all just play for the love of the game, but there's some real talent around too. My first baseman played in the minors, same for the shortstop. All four of our outfielders played college ball, and our one other pitcher, like me, even made it to the big leagues for a half-season or so. So while we're out here for fun, we take it seriously once the ump says "play ball."

It was at the end of one halfhearted wind sprint that I stopped for a moment to look out past the left field foul pole toward the little harbor there and the bay beyond.

It was an absolutely perfect, blue-sky day, the way it can be in Florida in the spring, the sun hot but not as deadly as it gets in July and August. Someone was out there in a rowboat, I noticed. I was happy for any excuse to stop and look for a minute or two instead of running those interminable halfhearted outfield wind sprints. You get to forty years old and getting into shape isn't the fun it used to be.

As I watched, the rise and dip of the oars and the boat's forward motion spent out a series of small whirlpools that bordered a peaceful wake, the bright sun bouncing off the tiny wavelets. It was mesmerizing, and I kept watching as the boat reached the dock and the guy inside tied it off, stepped out, started walking from the dock across the two-lane street to where I stood at the ballfield's low fence.

"You're playing base ball?" he asked. He looked a little lost.

I nodded, added, "Yes. We're a semipro team, just play for fun."

He was thin, under six feet tall, had a small moustache, wild dark hair parted right down the middle and then pulled back behind each ear. He brushed back that dirty hair. "You need a player?" he asked. "I play a pretty decent catcher."

"Well," I hesitated. We had a lot of guys who tried out for the team, but the truth of the matter is that most people just can't play the game. We weren't some fantasy camp, where they coddle wannabes and give them uniforms and a chance to pretend. This wasn't slow-pitch softball where everyone's a hitter and anyone can play. This was baseball. Hardball. The real thing.

But, on the other hand, we could always use a guy who could handle himself behind the plate. Truth was, nobody our age seemed to want to put on the tools of ignorance for more than a few innings, so this guy was worth a look. "Sure," I said, "c'mon on in and give it a shot."

And he did. And within the hour I knew we had the new catcher we needed. He was a natural, with a bullet arm, a great glove; a singles hitter but he always made contact.

He called himself Steve Crane, and I thought that was pretty funny, rowing up in an open boat and all that.

And then I realized he really meant it.

5

HER BLUE HOTEL

I met Emily in Paintsville, Kentucky, my first year in professional ball. She was drop-dead gorgeous and bored to tears in that tiny town, a prom queen turned part-time student at the local junior college while she worked for her daddy's insurance business. I was a star at that level of the game, and there was no competition in Paintsville. It took us something like ten minutes to go from hello at the Blue Hotel bar to oh, yes, back in my little apartment. She was the most beautiful girl I'd ever seen, and if the sex wasn't that good, the looks were compensation. I saw her as the perfect ornament. She saw me as her ticket out, her lifetime pass to the big leagues, and that was okay by me. Hell, I saw me headed that way myself, and she made for one great-looking baseball wife, all perfect blond hair and those tight jeans and that luscious accent, y'all.

But then I didn't quite become the ballplayer she'd figured on. Or the famous sportscaster either, though I gave that a try for a few years. Or even, later, the Famous Writer.

I didn't become much of anything and one day, five years into the marriage—she was patient with me, I'll give her that—I came home to packed bags and a note about what I hadn't turned out to be. Later, I found out she had a boyfriend who made more money than he knew what to do with in software sales, so Emily finally found somebody who could succeed at something, and that gave her a chance for a new beginning. That's how she told me to see it in that note: A New Beginning.

6

A GIRL OF THE STREETS

Cora wanted to know about my writing. It started with the how-many-words-a-day questions and went on from there, growing in complexity, some of them personal and some of them about the work. She wanted to be a writer herself and kept talking about how she was willing to pay her dues to get there. I should have thought that through a little better when she said it. She had stories to tell, God knows. I found out this: she was a local girl, Catholic elementary school at St. John's Parish out on the beach. Then four years at St. Petersburg Catholic High School, where she played on the softball team and edited the yearbook. She was a good Catholic girl from a solid family—father a pediatrician, mother a teacher, two little brothers who played soccer. She was on her way to wherever it is good Catholic girls go for their careers when she got hooked up in college to a boy with the wrong kind of dreams and the wrong way to reach them, and she found herself in trouble—drugs and pregnant and the boyfriend got mean. I didn't get all the details, but there was no child and a nasty little scar on the backside of that gorgeous left cheek.

So she'd come back from all that. Back in school, wanting to write, looking great. And paying her way through as a dancer at the Club De Dream out on the beach. I started going there every Tuesday and Thursday night. She went on at ten, this good Catholic girl, and oh, my.

7

A SENSE OF OBLIGATION

Halfway through the season I had a terrible Sunday pitching, getting roughed up for nine earned runs on the way to losing 15–2. We have a ten-run mercy rule in this league, and it was a good thing for us, since it ended the game early. Most of us went to the Little Regiment bar afterward, a dark wood-paneling faux-British pub not far from the field. A few pints of Guinness sounded pretty good to me at that point.

We weren't in there more than fifteen minutes when Cora left to play some pool with Humphrey Regis, our shortstop. He was fresh from a recent tough divorce and had been oh for four at the plate, so a little eight-ball with Cora must have seemed heaven sent.

That left me and Steve alone at the table for a few minutes. Steve pulled my collection out of his bag and told me he'd read it.

I stared at him.

"This is the copy you signed for Cora," he said. "She asked me to read it."

I nodded.

"It's good work," he said. "I like it. But." He gave me a slight smile. "I know a little something about writing, David. I did well at it there for a while."

I nodded. "Sure. I know. You're Stephen Crane, *the* Stephen Crane."

He shrugged those thin shoulders. "You know what I mean, all right, David." He leaned back in his chair, sipped on his beer. "Look. David, I don't know how or why this is happening either, chum. I think I recollect something that Herbert said, about that machine of his."

"Sure," I said again. "H.G. Wells and his time machine."

He laughed. It sounded bitter. He started to rise. "All right, then, David. I'm sorry I tried to monkey with this. Cora thought you'd appreciate my advice, that I should try and help your career."

"Cora thought?" I shook my head, waved at him to sit back down. "Please, Steve, stay. Look, I appreciate what you're trying to do, really, but my career is fine. Just about got my novel done, and my agent says she's close on the next deal. I might get to quit teaching if things really take off, you know."

"Bully for you, David," he said. Then he smiled at me. "David, can I tell you a story?'

"Sure," I said. "Tell me a story. Something about the Civil War, right? About red badges, about fighting and dying and all that."

I knew that sounded mean even as I said it. This poor guy really did think he was Stephen Crane; he'd convinced me that he really believed that, at least. And here I was teasing him, acting like I was hot stuff just because I'd written a few books and won a few awards.

He was staring at me. I tried again, nicer. "I'm sorry. Sure, absolutely, I'd like to hear a story.

He shook his head slightly. "The 'Red Badge,'" he said, then paused for a moment. "You know, I'd never seen war when I wrote it."

I nodded. "I knew that."

"I thought I could tell the truth about war when I wrote it. I thought I had some talent."

"You did, on both scores."

He shook his head again. "No, not really. You know, it's hard for a man to realize these things about himself." He paused, sipped on his beer, went on. "I didn't know the truth from an electric streetcar. I came to realize that in May of 1897, the Greco-Turkish War. The *New York Journal* hired me as a correspondent, and it was there, at Velestino, that I finally saw the truth of it."

He smiled, shrugged. "Death is very real." He took a sip of beer, smiled again. "I wonder how close to the truth I might have come if I'd lived past twenty-nine."

"Now you'll get to find out. You're writing, aren't you?"

He shook his head. "No. That's the rum thing. There's no time."

"No time? We practice a couple of times a week and we play a single game on Sundays. What are you doing with the rest of your time?"

He frowned. "What am I doing?" There was a long pause. "I don't know," he said. "I'm trying to think about it right now, trying to remember, and I don't know. When I'm not at the park, playing the game, it's all gray, blank."

"Oh, c'mon." The poor guy, I thought, was Looney Tunes. "You're here now, with me, and there's nothing gray."

"Yes, I am at that." His eyes widened. "Maybe it's you, David. Maybe it's you that's brought me back, you that makes me real."

I laughed. "Right. Me and my magic powers, that's it. Okay, then, here," and I grabbed the paper placemat from under his plate, flipped it over to the blank side, pulled my antique Waterman pen out of the reading glasses case where I keep it, and handed it to him, calling his bluff. "Abracadabra, Steve. Here's your chance. Get writing. I'll just hang out here and make you real for a while as you scribble."

He chuckled. "It might work at that, my friend," he said. He held up the pen to look at it—an 1893 Waterman #25, eyedropper filled, a classic with a tapered cap and gold-filled bands around the barrel. Emily splurged and bought it for me to celebrate my first contract.

He gave me the damnedest look, part smirk, part wonderment, then reached over to put his finger on the placemat, slid it back his way, and started writing. I shut up and for the next hour I just sat there and watched him write. It was my job to keep the beer coming for both of us.

His handwriting looked clean and legible, but I couldn't read it from where I sat, beyond being able to see that it was prose. He wrote steadily; the motion of pen against the paper was so fluid, so constant, that I could see the story taking shape before my very eyes. There was no hesitation, no long moments where he was lost in thought, no getting up to wash the dishes or cut the front yard and vacuum the carpet or stare out the window or any of the other tricks I used myself to stall for time in the middle of a writerly panic. It was utter confidence at work— dumbfoundingly utter confidence.

As he got toward the end of the first placemat page, he coughed, the first one I'd heard from him in the couple of months he'd been around. It was just a sharp, quick bark, that first one; but a few minutes later came another and then another, each one looser than the one before, like his lungs were filling with mucus right there in front of me. Finally, an hour into that writing session and on his fifth placemat by then, the cough was so rattlingly hard that he had to stop and get it over with. I got up from my chair and came around the table to help him but he waved me away, then grabbed one of the big paper napkins from their holder on the table and held it to his mouth as he brought the mucus up. He spat into it finally, and his lungs seemed to clear. He tossed the napkin back on the table and went back to writing as I sat back down. Later, when the waiter came by to clear away the empty

beers and the used napkin, I saw the red stains on the paper
napkin.

The coughing eased after that; there were still some fits but
nothing so dramatic as that one, and then, finally, he seemed to
hit a stopping point. He set the pen down, leaned back in his
chair, reached over to pick up his beer, and took a good, long
pull. He smiled. "You, of all people, must understand just how
good that felt, David."

"That's a hell of a cough," I said.

He waved my concern away. "No, not that. The writing. It
was ..." he searched for the right word, "it was real; do you
know what I mean?"

"Sure," I said. But I didn't. Not then.

"David, everything's square with us, right?"

"Sure."

"Then I wonder," he started to say, but then he fell into that
cough again, a quick bark that built to a loose rattle that he
covered with another big paper napkin, his whole body
convulsing with it.

"You ought to get that looked after," I said.

He laughed, and that brought him to a cough again for a
minute. Then he smiled, nodded. "Yes. Get it looked after.
Damnable thing."

Then he reached over to take my hand. Holding on to my
hand, gripping it tighter as he spoke, he said this: "David. Why
are you playing base ball? A fellow your age ... you're the oldest
chap on the team by a good ten years—you could be hurt, pull a
muscle, break an ankle. It doesn't make any sense really, does it?"

"No, I suppose it doesn't."

"But you're playing."

I smiled. "Yes. I'm playing."

"Why?"

I thought about it, started tossing out reasons, possibilities,
excuses. "Hanging on to my youth? Getting some exercise? Still
learning to hit a curve? Hell, I don't know. Because I enjoy

myself. Because I can quit worrying about other things when I'm out there pitching."

"What do you think about when you're on the mound?"

"The game. The situation. The next pitch. Whether or not my catcher can throw that runner out at second."

He smiled, the cough gone. "To the last question, the answer would be yes, old chap."

It was my turn to laugh. "I don't know. I play because I love it. There's no excuses, nothing gray out there. I pitch, and they hit, or they don't, that's it. At the end, it's all very definite, very real."

"Real?"

"Yes, real. I can feel the ball, the glove, the rubber, and the hole I've dug with my right foot in front of it; the downslope of the mound, the feel of the ball's stitches against my fingertips, the way it comes off the side of the knuckle of this finger," I held up the second finger of my right hand, "when I throw a curve, or off this spot," I touched a spot a little higher up on that same finger, "when I throw a slider. It's all about physical sensations and concentration, lovely, lovely concentration. It's reality. Unarguable reality. I love it for that."

He nodded. "Unarguable reality. I like that." He leaned back in his chair, put his hands behind his head, and said this: "Art—your art, my art—is involved in that terrible war between lies and the truth, David, and the truth must win out. Describe it truthfully. Make it real. That's all I wanted to say."

He leaned forward. "If you're truthful about the surface, if you get the details right, then the interior is revealed and you can get close to the bone, get inside the bone, to the marrow, and tell the truth. That's all. This is something that took me years to figure out. Only at the end, lying there at Brede one day in the sun, dying, knowing I was truly dying, did I finally begin to figure it out. And then it was too late."

He let go of my hand, took the paper mats he'd been writing on with tiny scribblings, folded them once, twice, and then put them into the pocket of his pants. He looked at me. "You have these skills, David. They're very impressive, just like your little speech about base ball."

"Thanks."

"But they're all a bit too, too ..." he hesitated, came up with the word, "too pyrotechnic. I can't find the truth of things in there anywhere. I don't see anything that really matters. That's all I thought I might say. All right?"

What was I supposed to say to that, to this man who thought he was an invention of mine, someone I'd brought to life, created from the ether? "Sure," I said. "It's fine, Steve. Thanks for the input. I appreciate it, really."

"All right, then," he said. And he got up and left, waving once as he walked out the door.

Okay, I thought as I finished off my beer, that would be irony, right? A guy like him, a guy who thinks he's a dead writer, preaching to me about telling the truth.

I set my empty beer glass down on the table, tossed a twenty on top of it, and went over to the pool table to shoot some eight-ball with Cora. Later, we headed back to my place at the beach, the one with the second-story deck that looks out over the dunes to the Gulf of Mexico so I can watch for the green flash that comes with some sunsets here. It's a bright emerald moment that shoots straight up from the final instant of the sun's disappearance into the Gulf. They're wonderful and rare and require concentration, focus, to see. Some people watch for decades and can't get the hang of seeing one. I'd seen a lot of them—dozens—over the years.

I wondered, as I got into my Lexus with Cora, if I'd ever get to see what Steve had written on those placemats. By this time, I'd read everything Crane had ever written. I'd know in a heartbeat if this guy was the real thing. I wondered about that all the way home. Later, the green flash was terrific. So was Cora.

8
_____

YELLOW SKY

"He was just trying to help you, David," Cora said to me on a Sunday morning a week later, the early light coming in the bedroom window to backlight her, so I couldn't see much of her face, just the penumbra of that long, blond hair around her, a vision, a miracle.

She rolled over on her side to face me, propped herself up on one elbow, shook her head to clear her hair out of her eyes. We'd argued about her telling Steve that I was a writer too. Now she wanted to explain herself.

"He likes you," she said, "and when I told him you were a writer, he said he'd like to see your work; that's all."

I stared at her. "You really believe it's him? You do know that Stephen Crane died in a sanitarium in Badenweiler, Germany, in 1900."

She stared back, slowly smiled. "So he's back from the dead, or some kind of ghost? I don't know, David. You tell me. You're the fiction writer. You're the one who makes all this stuff up."

I played along. "I wonder how he got here, then," I said. "He keeps talking about H.G. Wells and his time machine. I looked it up to make sure. *The Time Machine* was Wells's first novel, that's all—an allegory about the British caste system in the Victorian Age."

"So what?" she said, leaning over to kiss me on my stomach. It tickled. Laughing, I pushed her back, then reached up to touch that perfect chin, run my fingers across those lips, as beautiful in the morning on their own as they were during the day when she'd put on her lip gloss and lined it in. She was young and perfect and I wasn't either one. And she'd actually bought a copy of my short story collection, which made her one of about a thousand people in the whole damn country. Part of me felt pretty awful about having an affair with a girl of twenty-two. But part of me felt I was not to be blamed. At least, with Cora, I was alive again. I was even writing again. Not particularly well, I thought, but bad words on the screen are better than no words at all.

I didn't know how long the bubble would last, floating along there in the metaphoric breeze with me inside it, playing these kids' games—sex with a twenty-something, baseball with a guy who claimed to be Stephen Crane.

Cora laughed. I watched those breasts move as she sat up on her knees and looked down on me. "You should get him to come guest lecture in your short story writing class. Now that would impress the students."

"They'd believe it was really him," I said. "All that stuff about Conrad and Ford Madox Ford and Henry James and all the rest —they'd lap that up. And the part about Wells and his time machine, they'd go crazy for that. All most of them want to write anyway is sci-fi and fantasy."

"He is pretty damn convincing," she said.

"And good looking too," I added, "in that dangerous kind of way."

She reached down to feel me. I was ready and she moved over on top, concentrating, her eyes closed as she eased on down. Then she opened her eyes—those perfect eyes—and smiled. "Yes," she said in a whisper, "he is kind of good looking and dangerous."

And then she started moving, up and down, and I started to lose control again.

That afternoon she came to the game to watch. It was the first time she'd done that. She didn't miss a single one after it. She even started keeping score.

9

ONE DASH—HORSES

The next game, Steve turned a single up the middle into a sliding double when the center fielder took his time fielding the ball and coming up to throw. Steve saw this as he rounded first and just kept going, sprinting hard for second. His slide was showy and maybe a little risky, spikes up pretty high, but he got in there safe and then I brought him in with a single of my own two pitches later. That moment, when he raced like a thorough-bred across the plate well ahead of the throw from left to score the tying run for us, was the second happiest I saw him in the six months he was here. His narrow face with that dour, scraggly, wild look on it finally lit up in a huge smile and he clapped his hands and shouted happily as he scored. His cough was gone. Never once in a practice or a game did I hear the faintest hint of that deadly rattle.

Later, in the dugout, he said this to me:

"I love running, lungs full of air and legs flying. It's an honest measure of a man, isn't it, David?"

I smiled at him, nodded. "Sure. An honest measure."

"You know, David," he said, crossing his legs there in the dugout and pulling out his pipe to suck on it dry, since the league rules didn't allow you to smoke. "You know, near the end, when the consumption had about claimed me fully there at Brede, Herbert would come visit."

"Herbert? Oh, H.G., right?" I said. "You know, he once said that 'The Open Boat' was an imperishable gem."

He smiled. "Really? Nice of him. That was a true story, you know."

I nodded. "The Commodore went down off the Florida coast. You were on your way to Cuba to cover the insurrection and you and the captain and a few others wound up in a lifeboat. You drifted just off the coast for a couple of days and then finally tried to ride it in through the surf. One guy died."

He smiled, nodded. "Close enough, David."

"And the month before that, waiting for the Commodore to be ready, you stayed in Jacksonville, Florida. That's where you met one Cora Stewart. She ran the Hotel de Dream."

He smiled. "She was stunning, David. A big ample bosom, that blond hair that she would loosen and let fall around her shoulders." He sighed. "I forgot everyone else."

"The drama critic for the *Chicago Daily News*?"

He nodded. "Amy Leslie. Lovely woman."

"But Cora?"

"Better. By yards, old chap, by yards and miles."

Then he went on. "Herbert would come visit Cora and I there at Brede, and he'd bring along a whole group of nieces and nephews so we could play rounders. I taught them how to play base ball instead. With a cricket bat and no gloves. That was the closest I came to base ball over there. Rounders, with a cricket bat." He shook his head, smiled again, and waved toward the field. "This, this splendid game. It's wonderful, David. You know that, right, how utterly splendid it is just to be out here playing base ball on a Sunday afternoon?"

I did know it, and told him so. You start to get a little older and suddenly things like a good hard slider down low and away, a hard-hit double off the wall, or even a scratch single up the middle—sure, they matter. Like making love to a beautiful woman in her twenties, like getting good reviews on your short story collection, like writing well and knowing you're in that zone: like all those things, it matters.

"Are you still writing?" I asked him.

He shook his head, then stood up, took in a deep breath through his nose. "What do you smell, David? Right now, take in the air and tell me what you smell."

I smiled, took a long, deep sniff. "Fresh air," I said, "and green grass."

"Leather," he said, holding up the glove I'd bought him, a good Rawlings catcher's mitt, an XPG 2000. "And sweat. And the dirt of the infield. I missed all this."

"Is it still the same?"

He laughed, picked up one of our metal bats—Louisville Slugger Terminator, thirty-four inch, thirty ounce. He held the bat up and laughed again.

"Yeah," I said, "me too. I miss the smell of the wood. We still had those wooden bats when I was a kid, you know."

He sat back down, slouched back against the bench. "It's close, old chap. It's nearly the truth. It smells like my childhood, like my father, the preacher, before he died. It smells like learning the game, throwing and catching and hitting out in the vacant lot next door. It smells like college, like playing for Syracuse and throwing out that Colgate man who was trying to steal. My God, I could play, David. I could really play."

"Why did you quit? Your health?"

He shrugged. "I suppose. Life. Death. My writing. Finding the truth. They all mattered too. And base ball is, after all, only a game."

"True enough."

"I'm on deck," he said, and stood, picked up the metal bat, walked out to the on-deck circle, and slipped the weighted doughnut over the barrel. I watched him as he took a few swings to loosen up. He was thin, but healthy; God, he glowed with it. Then Tommy ground out and it was Steve's at bat again. He turned once to look at me, smiled, and then stepped into the batter's box. Two pitches later he slapped a single up the middle. The look on his face as he stood there at first, happy with another base hit, held some essential truth, I knew, something real.

10

THE MONSTER

I've lied about a lot of this. I drive a gray Honda Accord, not a Lexus. I've never seen the green flash at sunset. Cora wasn't really that good looking, or that young, or even a student. She didn't dance at the Club De Dream; she worked in customer relations for the phone company, and she was well into her thirties if she was a day; and her breasts sagged and she hadn't read my short story collection and she didn't flirt with me and we never made love. My earned run average in the big leagues was really 7.50. I was only up for one game, not one month, and I got ripped by the Mets for three very long innings. In fact, I was never in the big leagues at all, but was lucky to spend three years in the lower minors, trying to get by with breaking balls. I never did have very good control.

My short story collection sold two hundred and fifty copies and the reviews were awful. My novel? In four years I've written about ten thousand words. Are they good words, at least? I don't know. I don't think so.

I make it all up. That's what fiction is, I thought, all lies. It's not real; it's safer than that; there's more distance.

Here's the truth about Emily, my ex-wife. She wasn't nearly

as good looking as I said, and she was a great deal nicer. In my second year of minor league ball, in Medford, Oregon, we had a baby, a perfect little girl, Annie, her hair as red as her mommy's.

A year later I was in Lakeland, Florida, playing A ball for the Lakeland Tigers in the Florida State League. It was ten in the morning and Emily was at work; her job as assistant manager at the Pancake House paid our bills while I struggled to find the strike zone. There was a fire in our apartment complex. I crawled in through a bedroom window and rescued Annie, but my face was ruined in the effort and by the time my wounds had healed, my baseball career was over, my wife and child had left. I wound up homeless. I died penniless at twenty-nine.

Or maybe it was this way: Emily was a hooker, working the streets of New York. I rescued her from that, and we had a child, a beautiful little blond Annie, and, for a while, everything seemed fine. But then I was let go by the Cardinal organization, and I couldn't find work, and Emily went back to what she did best and little Annie died and Emily was murdered by her pimp and I was a crackhead and I died, penniless, in the gutter, at age twenty-nine.

Or, no; our child was abducted and I found her, dead, in the woods, her body placed against the rotten trunk of a downed tree that lay in a bower, her body framed by the overhanging branches so that the autumn sun came through like cathedral lighting. There were ants on her face, crawling in and out her nostrils, the empty sockets of her eyes. I was shattered by that sight. No, I was the murderer, and I turned myself in and I was executed in Florida's Old Sparky, smoke rising, sparks flying, the smell of burnt flesh. I was twenty-nine.

No. We were all in a small boat together. Me, my wife, our daughter, adrift after our cruise ship sank off the coast of Florida. We could see the shoreline, huge breakers rolling in just a few hundred yards away, so big we didn't dare try to get through them to safety. Finally, exhausted, we had to try. I made it and dragged Annie to safety; but Emily ... poor Emily drowned, and I've never forgotten the look on her face, the rage of it, as she slipped away. She wanted so badly to live. It broke my heart. She was twenty-nine.

No. Those are all lies too, of course. Here's the real truth:

My father was an agent for Farmer's Insurance in Edwardsville, Illinois. He was good at his job. Mom taught English at Ward Junior High. We had a good life there, me and my brother and sister. I played Little League and we won more than we lost. I went to Mary, Queen of Peace for grade school and survived the nuns, then Edwardsville High School where I played football, basketball, and baseball for the Tigers and did fine. Then off to major in English at Southern Illinois University, where I discovered Crane, and myself, and a good changeup that got us to the Division II national championship game, where we lost to Cal Poly when I gave up a scratch single to their worst hitter at the wrong moment.

My two best friends went to Iraq while I played baseball in college. One of them came home alive; the other in a box. I didn't sign up with them. Instead, I started that minor league career, which stayed minor league in writing, in life. I married a nice girl. We have a nice family. I have nice degrees from nice colleges and did a nice master's thesis on the truth in Stephen Crane's fiction. I teach at Pinellas County Community College, where I'm head of the creative writing program. I've sold exactly three short stories—one to the online version of the *Mississippi Review*, one to *Elysian Fields*, and the third to *Alabaster*. That makes me well published by community college standards. I make a nice living. When I write, I really use that antique Waterman that Emily bought me. It connects me, somehow, to the man I studied so much.

I play baseball on weekends with some other nice people. We lose more than we win, but I'll be damned if it isn't fun. Just like Steve said, it's an honest measure of a man, this splendid game. When you face a good hitter, when you're at bat facing a hard slider, when that sharp grounder comes your way or that sinking liner loops toward you in right—you can't hide; you can't lie; you can't fake it. You make the play, or you don't. Reality sounds pretty boring, doesn't it? But that's it; that's me; that's the truth of it.

11

A NOTEBOOK

And there's this too: Stephen really did come rowing in that Sunday in May. He tied up his rowboat and walked over to watch us and we gave him a glove and a ball and a bat and, my, he could play The Game. We finished with two wins and twelve losses the season before he came. We won ten this past season, with Steve catching and hitting third. He made me a better pitcher. I learned things from him, some of them about baseball.

I looked up his stats, which is what we do in baseball. He played in the Knickerbocker League for the New Jersey Athletics. They played at the Elysian Fields. He gave the professional game five good years before he turned to writing for a living, where he finally made a lot of money and married a rich, young socialite named Cora Stewart. They moved to England, where he became a real man of letters and lived a long, productive life.

No. I lied about that. He played baseball for Lafayette College his freshman year and at Syracuse University the next year, where he said, "The truth of the matter is that I went there more to play base ball than to study." That's the way they spelled the game in those days, like two words. I want this to be accurate.

He flunked out of Syracuse, drifted into purposeful poverty

in the Bowery, and emerged from there with a self-published short novel, *Maggie: A Girl of the Streets*. That got him the chance to do more, and so he wrote *The Red Badge of Courage* and became famous, if not rich.

The Red Badge was in 1894. In 1897, a famous writer at age twenty-six, he met Cora Stewart, already thirty years old and a failed socialite who ran a discreet bordello, the Hotel de Dream. They fell in love. He truly did survive the sinking of the Commodore and wrote a news story that became a short story that is generally said to be the best thing he ever did—and every word of it a kind of truth: "The Open Boat."

Three years later he was dead, his frail lungs doing him in. Those last few years he traveled as much as he could, but called England his home. Henry James, Ford Madox Ford, Joseph Conrad, H.G. Wells—they all loved him and his work. They thought him important. In 1899, he declined rapidly. They sought a cure in Germany. Cora was with him at the end. You can look all this up if you don't trust me, and I wouldn't blame you.

And this is the truth too: there really was a rainbow that last day in September, and those dark clouds to the east over the gray chop of the bay, and that small rain that down could rain to soak me, sneaking up on me until I realized, at game's end, that the rain, my sweat, the lies, my curveball, my lack of control was, all of it, a lie, that nothing was real except, maybe, Stephen and his stories and Cora, his and mine, there in the stands.

12

WOUNDS IN THE RAIN

In the top of the ninth of that final game, Steve got me through it and I slowly found my control again. I let in enough damage that they tied the score, but we answered with a run in the bottom and then all I needed was three outs in the top of the tenth.

I was so tired, so hot and wet that I couldn't think straight. Steve, behind the plate, was calling the pitches. I trusted him completely. We were up by that one run and I had no relief. Slider, slider, slider to the first guy and he went down swinging on all three, thank God. One out.

The next guy up had hit a double in the seventh and here he was again. Okay, then, slider wide, slider inside, fastball down the middle and he ripped it—another double, this one into the corner in left.

Steve came clanking back out again. "Got that one up," he said.

I nodded.

"I'd like to win this one, old chap, wouldn't you?" he asked.

I was too tired to care, but you can't say that to your catcher. "Sure," I said. "Let's get two more outs and we'll all go home happy."

"Yes, that's it," he said. "Everyone goes home happy." And he grinned at me, tossed me the ball.

This is probably what happened after that. I came in with a slider again, low and inside, but the guy went down and got it, drilled it right down the line. Foul.

Another slider, over the plate some more, and a hard groundball, but right at Randy Miller, our first baseman. He fielded it cleanly and stepped on the bag while the runner moved over from second to third.

Two outs and a man on third. Okay, more tired sliders, then; Steve with his two fingers stabbing at the red dirt behind the plate. Ball one. Strike one.

And then, like I meant it, like I could pick my spots like that, like I had that kind of control over my pitches, over myself, my life, I came in with a good pitch, low and outside. Strike two. Steve, back there, shook his fist at me, good pitch.

Same call, same pitch and the guy hit a two-hopper right back at me. I gloved it, pulled it free, tossed it to first and that was that. We win. Season over. First damn place for the first damn time in the five years I'd been playing again.

No. Same call, same pitch, and the guy hit a two-hopper right back at me. I gloved it, pulled it free, and threw it fifteen feet over my first baseman's head. Runner scored from third. Game over. Season over. We lost. We came close, but we lost. I lost.

It was raining, I realized. It had been raining lightly for two innings and I hadn't noticed until the game ended and the rain started coming down harder, with a distant flash of lightning and a rumble of thunder.

I walked over to shake hands with the other team, like we always do in this league. Nice game, I told them, which was true. Good job, they told me, and there was some truth in that too.

I got back to the dugout and Steve wasn't there. I looked in the stands. Cora was gone. I dropped my glove into my athletic bag and saw some paper folded in there. Those placemats. His scribbling. The antique Waterman I'd loaned him was clipped to the folded sheets, holding them together.

I pulled the pen free, opened the pages. The first page had this on it in that careful handwriting of his:

None of them knew the color of the sky. Their eyes glanced level, and were fastened upon the waves that swept toward them. These waves were of the hue of slate, save for the tops, which were of foaming white, and all of the men knew the colors of the sea. The horizon narrowed and widened, and dipped and rose, and at all times its edge was jagged with waves that seemed thrust up in points like rock.

That's the opening passage from "The Open Boat." I looked at the second sheet. It began like this:

The great Pullman was whirling onward with such dignity of motion that a glance from the window seemed simply to prove that the plains of Texas were pouring eastward. Vast flats of green grass, dull-hued spaces of mesquite and cactus, little groups of frame houses, woods of light and tender trees, all were sweeping into the east, sweeping over the horizon, a precipice.

That's the opening passage from "The Bride Comes to Yellow Sky."

I looked at the next sheet and it was the opening from "The Blue Hotel." All that writing that day, I thought, all of that just copy work, scribbling down what he'd already done. I shook my head, tossed those first three sheets back into the athletic bag. Held the fourth and fifth in my hands, looked at them.

And didn't recognize them.

I'd read every story that he'd ever written and this one wasn't among them. He'd been editing on it; you could see the scratched-out words and their replacements, see whole lines scratched out and rewritten. My hand started shaking as I read it. I got dizzy, then steadied myself, put those precious pages and the pen he'd used back into the athletic bag, then walked out of the dugout and stood there for a few minutes, looking up to feel the rain on my face.

13

LAST WORDS

Okay, then, this is the truth as I know it: we lost, but losing is part of winning and they both are part of what's real. Maybe I threw that ball away on purpose so Steve wouldn't be able to let it go at that, so he'd be back in February when we start the next season. Maybe he'll have Cora with him, and maybe Conrad, so I can finally find out what he thinks of The Game. They'll show up that first practice, rowing into the harbor in that little boat, emerging from the haze and fog of February's heat over cold winter water. I'll walk over there, and say hi, and help them out of the boat, help them tie it up to the dock.

And then we'll play catch, take a little infield, some batting practice, catch a few fly balls, and just play the game, loosening up for the season to come, ready to find whatever realities, whatever truths, there are out there on the diamond. I think maybe it will happen that way.

At that moment I stood there, face wet in that cool spray. Then I walked over to the low fence, hopped it, and jogged to the harbor. The open boat was just thirty yards away, heading toward the gray sheets of rain sweeping in from the bay. Steve was in it, rowing. I could see the happy smile on his face. It was the happiest I ever saw him. Cora, there with him, turned around to look at me. I raised my hand. They both raised theirs, and then they waved, and then the rain came down harder and the gray closed in and they were gone.

AUTHOR'S NOTE

Like a lot of writers, I admire the short stories of Stephen Crane, who died much too young at age twenty-eight in a health spa in Badenweiler, Germany, where he'd gone with his common-law wife, Cora, to seek treatment for his tuberculosis. In this work of fiction I have played fast and loose with Crane's life and his baseball skills; but he really did play baseball at Syracuse, where he was a catcher and a shortstop with a batting average of .272 and a passion for the game that was greater than his love for his studies. After an embarrassing loss to Colgate, Crane dropped out of Syracuse and headed to New York to start his writing career. Some years later he met Cora Stewart and they fell in love. She was with him when he died. Perceptive readers will notice I pay my respects to his stories in the section titles of "Stephen to Cora to Joe."

—Rick Wilber, June, 2020

ACKNOWLEDGMENTS

We owe immense gratitude to the editing acumen of Sheila Williams of Asimov's Science Fiction magazine, who not only liked "The Wandering Warriors" enough to buy it, but gave it the cover for her May/June 2018 issue. Thanks are also due to Alejandro Colucci for the outstanding cover art that resulted, and we're very happy that he graciously agreed to its use for this WordFire edition.

Our thanks and deepest appreciation go to Kevin J. Anderson, Rebecca Moesta, Marie Whittaker, and the entire WordFire team for this wonderful book edition of "The Wandering Warriors", and the two additional stories reprinted with it.

Finally, and as always, we're grateful to our agents, Robert G. Diforio of the D4EO Literary Agency (Rick), and Caitlin Blasdell of Liza Dawson Associates Literary Agency (Alan).

ABOUT THE AUTHORS

Alan Smale writes alternate and twisted history, historical fantasy, and occasional pure SF. His novella of a Roman invasion of ancient America, "A Clash of Eagles", won the Sidewise Award for Alternate History, and his series of novels set in the same universe, *Clash of Eagles* (2015), *Eagle in Exile* (2016), and *Eagle and Empire* (2017), is available from Penguin Random House/Del Rey. Alan has also sold more than forty pieces of shorter fiction to *Asimov's*, *Realms of Fantasy*, *Abyss & Apex*, and numerous other magazines and original anthologies, and his non-fiction science pieces about terraforming and killer asteroids have appeared in *Lightspeed*.

Alan grew up in Yorkshire, England, acquired degrees in Physics and Astrophysics from St. Edmund Hall, Oxford University, and then moved to the US in his late twenties. He currently performs astronomical research into neutron stars and black holes at NASA's Goddard Space Flight Center in Greenbelt, MD, with more than a hundred published academic papers, and serves as director of a data archive that contains the complete datasets from dozens of astronomical satellites and experiments. In what is laughingly referred to as his "spare time," he also sings bass with high-energy vocal band The Chromatics and is co-creator of their educational AstroCappella project, spreading astronomy through *a cappella* in schools across the country. The Chromatics have been Music Guests of Honor and regular performers at many SF conventions across the north-eastern US, which gives Alan yet another excuse to hang out with fellow science fiction writers and other really cool people. Check out his website at AlanSmale.com, or follow him on Face-book/AlanSmale or Twitter/@AlanSmale.

Rick Wilber's award-winning stories that merge baseball and the fantastic are published regularly in *Asimov's Science Fiction* magazine and other magazines and antholo-gies, with some two dozen of the baseball-influenced stories in print. The stories often feature Rick's alternate history version of the famously intelligent baseball player and spy Morris "Moe" Berg, sometimes called "The Professor" for his Ivy-league degrees and ability to speak a dozen languages. In our reality, Berg was a catcher who became a spy for the OSS in World War II and helped thwart the Nazis' plans for an atomic bomb. In Rick's imagination, Berg and his friends travel through multiple reali-ties to fight fascism. Or, in the case of "The Wandering Warriors," to have some fun teaching the ancient Romans the game of baseball. One of Rick's Moe Berg stories, "Something Real," won the Sidewise Award for Best Alternate History— Short Form in 2013, and another, "The Secret City," was runner-up for the award in 2019.

Rick has published a half dozen novels and short story collections, including the recent *Rambunctious* from WordFire Press. Other books include several college textbooks on writing and the mass media, a memoir about his father's life in baseball, and more than fifty short stories in major markets.

The son of a major league baseball player and coach, and a three-sport college scholarship athlete himself, Rick often incorporates sports into his fiction. He is a Visiting Professor in the low-residency MFA in Creative Writing at Western Colorado University, and he is the co-founder and co-judge with *Asimov's Science Fiction* magazine editor Sheila Williams of the Dell Magazines Award for Undergraduate Excellence in Science Fiction and Fantasy Writing, awarded annually at the International Conference on the Fantastic in Orlando, Florida.

He lives in St. Petersburg, Florida.

His website is rickwilber.net.

IF YOU LIKED ...

If you liked *The Wandering Warriors*, you might also enjoy:

Four Unpublished Novels
by Frank Herbert

Typhoon Time
by Ron S. Friedman

Clockwork Lives
by Kevin J. Anderson and Neil Peart

OTHER WORDFIRE PRESS TITLES BY
RICK WILBER

Rambunctious

Our list of other WordFire Press authors and titles is always growing.
To find out more and to see our selection of titles, visit us at:

wordfirepress.com